Arthur Sketchley

Mrs. Brown and Disraeli

Arthur Sketchley

Mrs. Brown and Disraeli

ISBN/EAN: 9783743358003

Manufactured in Europe, USA, Canada, Australia, Japa

Cover: Foto ©Andreas Hilbeck / pixelio.de

Manufactured and distributed by brebook publishing software (www.brebook.com)

Arthur Sketchley

Mrs. Brown and Disraeli

Mrs. Brown and Disraeli.

BY

ARTHUR SKETCHLEY,

AUTHOR OF "THE BROWN PAPERS," "MRS. BROWN ON THE ROYAL RUSSIAN MARRIAGE," ETC.

LONDON:

GEORGE ROUTLEDGE AND SONS,

THE BROADWAY, LUDGATE.

THE "MRS. BROWN" SERIES.

BY ARTHUR SKETCHLEY

———◆———

One Shilling each, fancy boards.

THE BROWN PAPERS. Reprinted from "Fun."

THE BROWN PAPERS. Second Series. Reprinted from "Fun."

MRS. BROWN AT THE SEA-SIDE.

MRS. BROWN'S VISIT TO PARIS.

MRS. BROWN IN THE HIGHLANDS.

MRS. BROWN IN LONDON.

MRS. BROWN AT THE PLAY.

MRS. BROWN'S 'OLLIDAY OUTING.

MRS. BROWN'S CHRISTMAS BOX.

MRS. BROWN IN AMERICA.

MRS. BROWN ON THE TICHBORNE CASE.

MRS. BROWN ON THE LIQUOR LAW

MRS. BROWN ON WOMAN'S RIGHTS.

MRS. BROWN ON THE TICHBORNE DEFENCE.

MRS. BROWN ON THE SHAH.

MRS. BROWN ON THE ROYAL RUSSIAN MARRIAGE.

And uniform,

MISS TOMKINS' INTENDED.

OUT FOR A HOLIDAY WITH COOK'S EXCURSION

MRS. BROWN AND DISRAELI.

—o—

PREFACE.

I says to Miss Pilkinton, "Don't talk to me about dreams not a-comin' true, for look at this 'ere Disreely a-comin' in a-flyin' right over Gladstin's 'ead, as 'oped for to get the better on 'im thro' 'is sudden disserlution; and me a-dreamin' three nights runnin' of three black cats on our back gardin wall, with their backs harches, and their tails like a bottle brush, a-swearin' frightful at one another, as is always a sign of friends a-fallin' out, with a secret enemy in the background; as is wot I always did consider that Disreely, tho', as I says to Brown, let 'im 'ave 'is innins, cos I'd dreamt of Gladstin a-standin' under the gallus, as is a sign of 'asty noose. Jest the same as a fire as I dreamt on for two nights arter the Pantecnicon were burnt, as scores 'ave lost their property in, and it's a mussy as Queen Wictorier didn't put 'er crown there along with them other jewels as she don't never wear now, to be took care on."

Miss Pilkinton she were rather in one of 'er jeery 'umours, so she says, "I wonder as you don't set up for a fortin'-teller with the cards, Mrs. Brown."

I says, "Cos I don't 'old with sich ways, as is pryin' into Providence, I considers," and that's 'ow it were as my own aunt come to marry a supercargo, thro' the knave a-turnin' up over the hace three times runnin', as the cunnin' man said, meant a fair man as 'ad crossed the sea, and would cross it agin, and so he did, pretty quick, when he'd collared 'er little bit of property, as she found out 'ad threw 'er over thro' bein' a married man, in both the East and West Injes, and a wife in Chiney besides.

And pinted 'im out to me years arter, a-settin' with a lot of Malays a-smokin' of 'is pipe at a open winder in 'Igh Street, Poplar, as put my temper up to give 'im a bit of my mind on the spot, over the airey railins, as threw the slop-basin over us, and got a crowd round the 'ouse and broke the winders, and 'ad the perlice, and then, poor thing, found out as she'd been and made a mistake, in indemni-fyin' the wrong man, thro' that party bein' a coloured mishunary, as bore a unblemished charac-ter, and 'ad took tea with the Bishop of Limus's own aunt the werry night afore, and 'ad only come

to Poplar, and were a-smokin' a friendly pipe for
to do good, and would 'ave brought a haction for
defacin' of 'is character, only Brown's lawyer
squared it for a fiver; so I don't 'old with cards,
but will stick to dreams, as ain't to be called
dreams, but is wisions, as clear as the night, and
reglar as clockwork; for I ain't 'ardly no sooner in
my bed than off I goes, and dreams enuf in ten
miuits to last all night.

And 'ave been warned in dreams, as I considers me a-bein' when I dreamt of bein' took
afore the magistret for tellin' fortins under false
pretences.

Cos there set the magistret all by hisself, a-
frownin' fearful at parties as was a-swearin' black
were white; and set there Queen Wictorier in 'er
weeds by 'is side, a-nudgin' on 'im with 'er elber
wot to ask, as said to me, " Why did you say as 'er
Grashus Majesty 'ad took and sent Prince Christshun to the Tower for not a-lettin' the Prince of
Wales shoot a rabbit in Winsor, as were wanted for
'is royal ma's supper."

I says, " Why, I never said such a thing, and as
to me a-sayin' as that there Prince Christshun 'ad
a wife aredy over in Germiny afore ever he come
'ere, why, it's jest wot I never did say, but stuck
up for 'im and took 'is part, and told Mrs. Padwick
as I didn't believe as Queen Wictorier weren't

more wide-awake in them Germin's ways than to
allow sich goin's on in 'er family."

Says Queen Wictorier, a-smilin' grashus,
"Right you are, Mrs. Brown, as 'ave ever been a
true friend to me and mine, as shan't never forget
your kindness in sending me that nightcap, when
my boy Wales were that ill."

"Ah!" I says, "Your Majesty, that's the
pattern for settin' up in comfort, and there's nobody but a mother as can feel for a mother."

"Do 'old your row," says a woice, as give me
a drive in the back with 'is elber; and that were
Brown, as said he couldn't close 'is eyes for me
a-talkin' in my sleep; but if that wasn't a true dream,
why then, all as I've got to say is, as nothink
ain't, for I'm sure I felt as much over that there
Prince's illness, as if he'd been my Joe; and what's
more, shows as wot goes on in sleep is beknown
to others, as is wot Miss Pilkinton and me 'ad the
words over; cos tho' she won't set down thirteen
to a meal any more than Queen Wictorier, as 'ave
been knowed to knock off a crowned 'ead a-comin'
to dinner, cos he'd make thirteen, and 'ave made
the Prince of Wales 'ave 'is dinner at a side-table
afore now, thro' 'im a-bein' one too many for 'er,
yet won't believe in dreams, and why ever not, is
wot I says, partikler as that impudent minx, Old
Sinful's servant, did take and summons me for

detainin' of 'er property, as she'd said as she'd give
me for tellin' 'er fortin,' 'er fortin, as was a base falsity, for she
come in a-cryin' 'er eyes out, a-sayin' as 'er mother's
bed would be took from under 'er, with the snow
on the ground, if she didn't pay three pounds
by twelve o'clock; and as she drored all 'er wages
of Old Sinful, and wanted a pound to make up the
money, and give me four old teaspoons to keep till
she brought it back. I didn't want the teaspoons,
but bought 'em on 'er out and out, and as luck would
'ave it, that gal of mine were a-listenin' at the door
and 'eard me say so, but turned out to be Old
Sinful's silver, as she'd been and boned, but 'owever was I to know that, so the magistret he took
and dismissed the summons, but ordered as them
teaspoons should be given up on Old Sinful a-
payin' me the pound, cos of it's bein' 'is own niece,
as it come out, as 'ad borrered the money of me, and
all lies about 'er mother's bed bein' took. But I
see all that in the grounds of my tea, as old Mrs.
Belcher showed me, as plain as the nose on your
face, tho' I larfed at it, when she took and turned
the cup round and round, and said as the grounds
not a-settlin' showed a somethink lurkin', and
then there certingly were four black bits by theirselves, and a long bit as she said were a thief, and
then fine dust-like at the bottom, as she said were
trouble to be got thro' and money out of pocket, as

I certingly were, for Old Sinful never give me back the money, and them spoons were that old, as I don't think they weighed much over a shillin' a piece. So there certingly is somethink in them tea-grounds more than meets the eye, but I never did think Mrs. Belcher a thief, tho' she were in the second-hand line, and is in Coldbath Fields now, thro' a silk umbreller and a gravy spoon, as she collared from a gentleman's 'ouse, where she were a-buyin' the lady's wardrobe, as 'ad 'er up in 'er bedroom, and took that mean adwantage, as 'ave come 'ome to 'er, a wile old cat, and fully accounts for my punch ladle with a guinea at the bottom a-disappearin', so in my opinion it's best never to sell nothink in the 'ouse, nor yet at the door neither, cos buyin' them flowers out and out is best, and not go a-swoppin' and changin', as always gets the wust of the bargain in the long run, as the sayin' is, as certingly is wot I always does. Brown he ain't one to give in to no superstitions, but even he's obliged to allow as my dreams is real, as the langwidge he'll break out with thro' 'avin' of 'is rest broke is downright dreadful in the dead of the night; and as I says to 'im, "Ah! when some on 'em comes true, parties will stare;" he says, "Oh! dry up with your rot." "Well," I says, "Brown, do listen to reason, and not go off to sleep agin, snorin' like a 'og in a 'igh wind, as the sayin' is, for I can take my solim davy as the black cat as knocked the other off the wall, were the image of Old Dizzy, the other as give a claw at 'im in fallin' were the image of Gladstin, as made 'is fur fly all over the place like a snow storm." But Brown, he didn't anser, so I says to 'im that werry next day at breakfast, I says, "Mark my words, if there ain't 'ot work somewheres afore the week is out," and sure enuf Gladstin took and dissolved suddin, afore Friday were over.

I reminded Brown on it, not as he's one to own as he believes, for he only says, "I wish as you'd go and dream along with Dizzy, and not break my night's rest with your row."

I says, "If you considers that a proper thing to say to your lawful wife, Mr. Brown, I don't; and shall keep my dreams to myself."

He says, "All right, and don't be a botherin' me with 'em."

I says, "I certainly will not, for," I says, "there's 'undreds as would 'ear about 'em with pleasure," let alone Mrs. Padwick, as when I've took arf 'er bed, would listen to me for ever, if she could 'ave kep' awake, as in the daytime she will; for she always says, "Well, Martha, what did Queen Wictorier say to you last night, and 'ow's Old Dizzy a-gettin' on?" and all like that.

So I always tries to remember my dreams for 'er

sake, and she wants me to 'rite 'em all down and send 'em to Queen Wictorier, as she says she's sure would like to know wot's a-runnin' in my 'ead all night.

And one thing I'm sure on, if she 'ad she wouldn't never 'ave gone to war with that there lot of niggers, nor yet 'ave tampered with our beer, as I consider is a touchin' every one in their werry wital pints, and 'ave upset Gladstin, as I knowed it would ; and so I said to Brown, I says, " Mark my words, if he don't get up to 'is neck in that liquor, and out of 'is depth too, as the sayin' is."

And then I should 'ave told 'er, as to edication, there's been a deal too much fuss about nothink, for as to thinkin' as they're a-goin' to make every one a scolard, they might as well try to make every one the same colour 'air and eyes, or all the same 'ight.

Depend on it, as some is made for to do one thing and some for to do another; and so long as they brings up children to honour their parents, and work 'ard, and keep out of the perliceman's clutches that's all as the most of us requires. And I'm sure as to religion, there's such a lot of 'em goin' about jest like Merryker, that parents is puzzled which to choose for theirselves, let alone a-thinkin' which they shall bring their children up in; and so it is as a-many ain't no religion at all.

And then I should 'ave said, as to free-trade I always were agin it, as is more free than welcome, as the sayin' is; and jest look at our mannyfacters as is downright ruined at it, and forriners a-cuttin' of us out and a-larfin' in their sleeves, as well they may, for they've got the pull all ways, sells all their goods to us free, and makes all our things pay.

Leastways, that's Brown's ways of lookin' at it, and he's a man with a long 'ead, as can see thro' a stone wall as far as anybody, as the sayin' is, and as to cheap bread and all that 'umbug, why, whatever is the use of the loaf only bein' fourpence if I ain't got the money to buy it.

No use a-'umbuggin' the poor man about cheap things when 'is wages keeps 'im at starvin' Why, it's jest for all the world like children without a 'apenny a-lookin' in at a pastrycook's winder and a-longin' for the tarts as they can't get.

No, I should say, give 'em plenty of work and good wages, and then there wouldn't be no relief wanted, as is the ruin of workin' people now-a-days; cos the moment they eats the bread of idleness thro' beggin' they wont work no more, and their sperrit is broke, and they ain't no proper pride left, and takes to drinkin' and all manner, and if I 'ad my way I wouldn't give a fardin' to any able-bodied man, but make 'im work or go to prison; as is where I'd precious soon send the lot as

'ave been in a conspiracy for to get that Wappin'
waggerbone off, and now as he's got not 'arf wot
he did ought to 'ave, they begins a-wimperin' and
a-sayin' let 'im alone; and as 'ow he were that nice
spoken party and quite the gentleman, and so he
is now, but with three aughts, as the sayin' is,
neither wit, money, nor manners; cos if he'd 'ad
wits he wouldn't never 'ave 'ad the impidence to try
on sich a game, as must 'ave been blowed on
sometime; and as to the money, them as give it
'im may whistle for it; and as to 'is manners, why,
'is own lawyer 'ave been and told us what they was,
and no wonder as that old black Bogey 'ave took to
'is bed with the weight as he must 'ave on 'is conshence, and let's 'ope as he've got that there gardin
injin, Miss Brains, for to nuss 'im, as will no doubt
get up a partition between 'em for to 'ave that there
injured innercent let out of prisin, and ask
parties to pity 'im; but in my opinion them as
pities such a feller is nearly as bad as 'im, as I wish
they'd flog 'im soundly hevery month of the four-
teen years, and then send 'im over to Horstralier to
'ave 'im tried agin for 'is goin's on in the bush, and
let 'is friends go over there now at once and wait
for 'im to come; and it's a pity as some of 'em as
is so fond on 'im ain't a-keepin' of 'im company
now, with their 'airs cut short and a-relishin' of the
skilly as he takes to so kindly.

Any'ow it must be a comfort for 'im to 'ave that lyin' waggerboue, Luie, along with 'im in Noogate, 'cos birds of a feather flocks together, as the sayin' is, and they can set and tell lies together whenever they meets, leastways, whenever they're allowed to open their mouths; and pre'aps they'll inwent another shipwreck; but it's my opinion as the next time as Luie 'ave the chance of savin' Ortin from death, it won't be from drownin', but pre'aps a bad fall thro' a rope a-breakin' with 'im, as weren't strong enuf to 'old 'im tho' tied tight round the neck.

I should say as Ortin must be precious wild at them as brought up this 'ere Luie for a witness, as must 'ave been downright fools to go and pick out a ticket-of-leave conwict, and then take 'im afore a judge.

But, as I were a-sayin', 'ang Ortin and Luie too, tho' I will say nothink don't prove wot dreams is plainer than me a-sayin' from the werry fust as that there 'og in harmour were Ortin; and as to 'em papers as says as he looks the gentleman all over, I should say they wasn't much judges of a gentleman; and as to 'is 'ands and feet bein' small, why, in course a shoulder-of-mutton fist would look small by the side of sich a porpus as that.

But, law, let the willin' rot in jail, as is 'is proper place, and let 'em as likes take and shed tears over 'im; and I'm sure as every respectable person is only too glad to get the waggerbone's name out of their mouth; and who cares 'ow he likes 'is skilly or 'ow he looks in 'is clothes; the only 'ard part as I considers is as we should 'ave to keep the wretch, as bread and water is too good for; but I certingly did know as he were Ortin, not only by dreams but on the cards, thro' the knave always a-turnin' up at the fifth letter, beginnin' with a O and endin' with a N.

Well then, didn't I say as that there Dook of Edinburrer would make a match in the Black Sea, as I see 'im a-swimmin' in three nights runnin'; and always said as the Prince of Wales would get over it from that night as I dreamed on 'im berried in plumes.

So I means to keep up my dreams cos there's no tellin' when they may come true, and then when things 'appens parties can't turn round and say whyever didn't you tell us, Mrs. Brown, as must 'ave dreamed on it the same as Maria Martin bein' murdered in the Red Barn, as I've knowed parties as lived near the spot, and the willin', if he didn't go and marry a schoolmissis as ought to 'ave knowed better, and not a good esample to 'er scholars to marry an adwertisement like that, as was took up over 'is own breakfast when bilin' a egg over the parlour fire; and it's a mussy as there wasn't no family, not as anyone would 'ave looked down on 'em if there 'ad been, cos in course they couldn't 'elp it; tho' there is some brutes as would 'ave throwed it in their teeth, as the sayin' is.

I'm sure that Gladstin must be glad to 'ave a bit of a 'olliday and take 'is good lady somewheres better than to Blackheath on a waggin, as is ways I don't 'old with, and wouldn't ride in a waggin among a lot of ruffs not to see Brown made Lord Mare.

But I don't suppose as Dizzy won't get to work much this side Easter as, in course, he keeps werry strick, tho' he ain't a Catherlic no more than this 'ere Duchess of Edinburrer, as no doubt must 'ave been a bit of a buster for Queen Wictorier for to 'ave on a wisit with nothink to talk but Rooshin, as, in course, Queen Wictorier knows; but I do 'ope as she won't go a tryin' to eat a candle jest out of perliteness, cos it 'ill make 'er 'eave 'er royal 'art up; as no doubt the Dook of Edinburrer made awful wry faces over it at fust, cos that's their ways in Roosher, as they all sets at table and eats their taller candles jest as Christshuns does sparregrass, and I've 'eard say as the Hemperor keeps 'is heye on 'em as wants to shirk, and 'ollers out, a-givin' a good gripe at 'is own dip, "Every true Rooshin eats 'is candle." So, in course, they must, tho' I 'opes as they've got a little somethink nice to take

after it; and any'ow I shouldn't care to dine with
'em thro' not a-'oldin' with taller in no shape, and
am sorry for Queen Wictorier, cos, in course, when
that there Hemperor of Roosher comes to see 'er,
it will be candles all day from mornin' till night,
and train ile to wash 'em down, as will be too rich
for the British Constitution.

I dessay as she's a werry nice young ooman, this
'ere Rooshin Doochess, but I don't care about 'er
name, as I consider Allysindrowner a mouthful to
call anyone by; but, pre'aps that's wot it is in
Rooshin, as may be short for somethink in French
as I do 'ope is the name as she'll go by.

I see some werry affectin' lines about 'er
a-comin' in the paper, but considerin' as she's a-
comin' by sea, it don't sound well as every werse
should end in "Drown 'er," they was rote by a
party in the name of Tenderson, or, as they calls
'im, the Lorryot, as is a nickname as they gives 'em
as rites werses, no doubt he's a werry pretty poet,
but give me Catnach for a ballid as 'ill bring tears
to your eyes; but even he couldn't make nothink
out of constant "Drown 'er."

So when you comes to think on it, Disreely ain't
got no sich time on it, a-'avin' to learn Rooshin and
eat candles, as in my opinion Gladstin 'ave been
and sneaked out on, cos tho' I've 'eard say he can
talk Greek jest as easy as Dutch; but then Brown

says as the Greek and the Rooshin wont never agree in the long run, cos 'em Rooshins wants to get 'old of the Greeks, so as they may collar that Turkey some day; but, as I says, let 'em Rooshins look out for they mustn't come no larks, cos if they do we shall be down their throats for all "the Drowners" as ever was inwented.

But, law! the older I gets the more I seems to get confused over all the 'ard names and goin's on as is all Greek to me; but Brown, he's that ropped up in 'is paper all the hevenin', as he reads bits on to me, and then busts out a-larfin' at me a-gettin' the 'rong pig by the tail, as the sayin' is; but 'owever can anyone take it all into their 'ead, I can't think; and as to who's in and who's out, it don't matter to me, only I should like to tell Disreely my mind over one or two things as was rocks as Gladstin took and split upon, as the sayin' is, as never would take my adwice any more than Old Sinful, as would go up them rotten steps of is'n and clean the back parlour winder with 'is own 'ands, as broke up like tinder under 'is wait and pitched 'im 'ead fust into the cowcumber frame, and might 'ave been layin' there now if I 'adn't put my 'ead out of our one-pair back, and see 'im 'eels uppermost a-strugglin', and give the alarm, tho' we wasn't on speakin' terms, and then for 'im to go and tell Mr. Bloxin, the doctor, as it were the shock of seein'

my ugly face popped sudden out of the winder as
made 'im nearly jump out of 'is skin as broke the
bit of clothes line as tied 'em steps together, as was
'is conshence, a old willin', cos the time afore. as I
put my 'ead out of that winder, it were to call
shame on 'im for draggin' of 'is granddorter up the
steps by the 'air of 'er 'ead, cos he cort 'er a-eatin'
of 'is currints, as is only thirteen, as he've got a
spite agin cos of 'avin' to keep the child thro' 'er
father bein' lost at sea, and 'er mother never one to
'old up 'er 'ead agin ; and that old beast, with 'is
old winegar-cruit of a dorter leads that gal a pretty
life, tho' she is 'er aunt, as certingly is a downright
sloven and as cheeky as our potboy; but then she
ain't never been larned no better, and as to manners I'm sure she ain't a patch on 'er grandfather as
is a reg'lar old 'og.

But to go back to dreams. I'm sure as mine is
reg'lar Nixin', the profit, over agin, as foretold that
there king a-goin' out a 'untin' as he'd be killed on
the spot, thro' a harrer a-comin' agin a tree; as I
suppose 'is 'orse took and shied at, or else tumbled
over it, as it's a shame for to leave sich things a-
layin' about, the same as Liza's 'usband and me
was werry nigh killed a-comin' 'ome in 'is shay-cart
thro' a cow as he drove over a-layin' in the middle
of the road one pitch-dark night, as couldn't 'ave
been in 'er right mind, I should say, for to go and

make 'er bed in a public thurrerfare, tho' pre'aps, poor beast, she thought it were the fields thro' the night bein' that dark as you couldn't see your 'and before you, as the sayin' is; not as cows 'ave got 'ands, tho' she 'ave 'eels like a Christshun, as some likes fried; and I'd dreamt of that cow the night afore, and never thought of mentionin' of it to Liza's 'usband, as would 'ave looked out sharper if I 'ad, not as it would 'ave made any difference, for if we 'adn't gone over the cow we should 'ave been pitched into the ditch, 'cos we'd got off the 'igh road into a by-path, so it were not the cow's fault arter all, as is a 'armless animal in a gen'ral way, though known to turn savidge for to purtect her calf, as is a mother all over?

I shan't forget that cow in a 'urry, for tho' no bones broke I never had a worse shake, and my welveteen jacket with a stain as big as a pancake in the middle of the back, as is no doubt wot I fell upon, as nothink won't take out, and Liza's 'usband he put 'is little finger out a-tryin' to save me, leastways he says so, but in my opinion not the man to put 'is little finger out to 'elp any one.

So that's why I keeps a reg'lar count like of my dreams, and if I'm took afore the School Board along of 'em, I shall glory in it. Cos they're true, and wot's true did ought to be stuck to, thro' fire and water, as the sayin' is.

But as to tellin' fortins with cards and sich like,
I don't 'old with it, tho' it certingly is singler 'ow
them things comes true as the cards shows for; but
the cunnin' man as did used to live close agin Lambeth Walk, I do believe as he were the old gentleman 'isself, a-livin' up in three-pair back, as he
could consult the stars more easier from, and cast
'orridscopes all over the grounds of Lambeth Pallis,
as did used once to stretch as far as Bedlim, but is
built over now, but was all fields when my dear
mother were a child, as would be nearly a sentry now
if livin', and 'er father were a carrier, and knowed
every hinch of the road from Westminster to Dul-
wich, as it took the 'ole day for 'im to get there and
back in them days, as always were armed for fear of
footpads, and remembered seein' Jerry Habershore,
the 'ighwayman, 'ung on Kennin'ton Common, as
blowed the 'ead off the last pot of porter as he ever
drank on 'is way to the gallus at the door of a
public in Newin'ton Butts, a-sayin' it were un-'ole-
some to drink it, tho' he 'adn't a 'our to live, as
shows the force of 'abits, as the sayin' is, as did
ought to 'ave been corrected in 'is youth, and then
wouldn't never 'ave come to that untimely hend, as
as I considers a gibbet; but as to bitin' off 'is
mother's ear at the foot of the gallus like Jack
Shepherd, it must 'ave been in 'is dyin' struggles, I
should say, and 'er a-goin' to give 'im 'er last kiss,

as ain't allowed now, any more than a-kissin' any
one thro' the railway winder with the train started,
as werry nigh were all over with Mrs. Twissell in
sayin' good-bye to Twissell, as were only goin' for
the day to berry 'is pardner, and if he hadn't
throwed 'is arms round 'er neck and 'eld 'er tight
agin the winder till the train were stopped, she'd
'ave been smashed to atoms, and, as it were, as
black as a coal in the face when they took 'er down
and fined her forty shillin's, as made Twissell forget
'isself and say as he wished he 'adn't never 'eld
'er.

So don't let nobody make light of dreams nor
yet trust to fortin-tellers, as is a month with 'ard
labour if caught in the fact, but three months if
they've done you out of money, tho' in my opinion
you deserves wot you gets for bein' sich a fool, the
same as that gal Mary Ann 'as 'ad her fortin told at
my own airey-door by a wile deceiver as walked off
with my second best tea-pot and Brown's boots, as
tho' only Britannia mettle, were quite good enuf in
the general way, partikler as them gals always will
put it on the 'ob, and 'ad only been brought
'ome the night afore, and three-and-sixpence to
pay for clumpin' 'em and twopence for the new
laces.

I were put out at that fortin-teller, as led to
werry unpleasant consequences, thro' me a-resolvin'

to punish the next one of the gang as I see about
the place; and so the werry next week I see a old
woman a-stoopin' down a-talkin' to the gal at the
kitchen winder jest as I turned the corner of the
street, as were a-gettin' dark.

So as it 'appened, a perliceman come up, and I
says to 'im, "There she is at it agin."

He says, "Who?"

"Why," I says, "a wile fortin-teller, as one on
'em 'ave robbed me a'ready."

"Ah," he says, "I'm on the look out for 'em,
as there's a lot about."

So we watched 'er up the steps, and see the gal
let 'er in, and then follers, and thro' me 'avin' the
key were in at the door afore she were out of the
passage.

So the perlice says, "I've got you, 'ave I! Oh,"
he says, "you ain't the party as robbed the safes all
down the road last week?"

She says, "Who dares say I am?"

Says the perlice, "This good lady told me as
you was a fortin-teller, in the 'are-skin cook line."

I 'adn't 'ardly got my breath thro' a-walkin' that
sharp to keep up with the bobby.

So I says to the gal, "Ain't this the party as
you give your ear-rings to, as promised you a new
sweet'art?"

Says the gal, "Law, no!"

Says the old woman, " My name is Melters, and I'll punish you for this, see if I don't."

I thought I should 'ave dropped, and says, " Oh, Mrs. Melters, mum !"

But she turns round on me and says, " I've 'eard on you afore, Mrs. Brown. You've been drinkin', as usual, and if it wasn't for your 'usban' bein' a decent man, I'd indite you for a noosance."

If it 'adn't been as the passage were too narrer, I should 'ave set down on the door-mat like a shot, for never in my life did I get sich a back'ander.

I tried to grasp out a few words, but she shoved by me and walked off, and the perlice too, a-sayin', " I think as you've been and woke up the 'rong passenger this time, old lady."

I couldn't speak, for that Mrs. Melter's 'usban' 'ad partikler busyness with Brown, as 'ad said to me, " Now, Martha, mind, if Mrs. Melters should come to see you, as you're partikler civil to 'er, and show 'er all the attentions as you can ;" for 'er 'usban' he owned a lot of 'ouse property all about, and the perlice, in course, knowed the name, and Brown were a-goin' to buy a 'ouse of 'em as were a bargin, and she 'ad been took up once on suspicion for shopliftin', as they said were a manier as she'd got, tho' nothink weren't proved agin 'er, so didn't punish 'er, tho', no doubt, if she'd been

a poor man's wife she'd 'ave got three months
at the werry least, as I'd been and said to Mrs.
Peltroe on the quiet, as works at 'er needle, and so it
got to Mrs. Melter's ears, as the sayin' is, and there
was a nice row, tho' I 'adn't never set eyes on 'er
in my life, and were goin' to law if Brown 'adn't
made it up thro' 'er 'usban', and she'd come for to
shake 'ands with me over it, as I 'adn't no ill feel-
ings agin 'er, and only 'eard the story thro' Mrs.
Gibson, as kep' the shop, and weren't certain as the
bit of hedgin' 'adn't fell by axcidence into Mrs.
Melters' muff, as she'd put on a chair close agin
the counter.

So in course it all looked agin me, and I 'ad to
'rite a 'umble apolergy, and that's why I don't like
no fortin-tellers, but they ain't the same as dreams,
as in my opinion did ought to be 'eld sacred, as the
sayin' is; and I'm sure that's wot I does with mine,
except when I tells 'em for anybody's good, as in
course would be any one's dooty, the same as poor
Mrs. Kirkland, as 'ad a dream as 'er next-door nay-
bour were found dead in 'is bed, and went and
knocked the family up at three in the mornin' to
see if it were true, and got nicely abused with a jug
of cold water throwed over 'er with 'is own 'ands,
as 'ollered out from the winder just as she'd told 'im
wot she'd come about, "Oh, indeed! you wait a
minit, and I'll show you as I ain't dead;" and

drenched her to the skin, poor soul, as meant well, and got the roomatics for 'er pains, as is wot comes of interferin' with your naybour's affairs, as is wot I never will do myself, not to my dyin' day, as the sayin' is.

MRS. BROWN AND DISRAELI.

—o—

I says to Brown, I says, "Don't talk to me about estendin' women's suffrages, indeed, for I'm sure they don't want them estended, as is 'it about and 'arf killed by them willins from mornin' till night, as only gets three months for it, and bound over for six, escept now and then when the magistret 'appens to 'ave a feelin' 'art, and will order 'em the cat, and that only thro' bein' a single man, as don't know 'ow aggrawatin' a woman's tung can be, like Mrs. Lister, as lived two doors off me, as I've 'eard 'er myself go on with my own ears at Lister by the 'our together till that time as he sent a flat-iron at 'er, as went thro' the kitchin-winder, and smashed the pot-boy's nose flat to 'is face, as were jest stoopin' down, poor feller, to 'and in Mrs. Challin's noonin's, as were there for a 'ard day's wash, as it was, with everything done at 'ome, and nineteen in family, includin'

the lodgers and twins, as makes a deal of work
to keep 'em clean and tidy; and if it 'adn't been
as Mrs. Challins 'ad 'ad the presence of mind to
straighten that young feller's nose out with 'er
finger and thumb, as brought it to its lawful shape
afore Mr. Polden's 'sistant took and strapped it
up that tight as he'd 'ave 'ad a nose flat to 'is
face like a thick-lipped nigger, as don't matter
for a black, and only looks nat'ral; but would
'ave been a dreadful defacement for a human bein'

So Brown, he give one of 'is grunts, and says,
"I wish to goodness they'd take and send you into
Parlyment, Martha, and then I should 'ave a little
quiet of a evenin' to read my paper in peace."

"Well," I says, "Mr. Brown, if you wants to
read in peace, I'm sure I can set with the gal, as is
a werry nice scolar, in the back kitchen, as is
boarded over jest like the front, and 'ave read a
good deal, and knows a many things more than
wot you might think, and that attentive to wot you
says to 'er, tho' she do get that confused in 'er 'ead,
and said as I told 'er as Gladstin 'ad 'ad sich a awful
fall thro' Disreely a-trippin'-up 'is 'eels, as they was
both a-goin' to see Queen Wictorier at Winsor, as
asked 'em to lunch in a friendly way, a little thinkin'
as they couldn't keep the peace, and as to me ever
a-sayin' as Disreely were the 'Igh Priest, and that
wild at findin' 'isself born a Jew boy as he took

and rote a lot of books for to prove as everybody else was Jews, why it's downright false ; I certingly 'ave been told it, cos in course I couldn't 'ave set and inwented sich a thing as that agin anyone in cold blood over my tea. Tho' Miss Brayim did say, when she were a-drinkin' tea with me, as the Jews was to reign werry soon, and that gal might 'ave 'eard 'er, for she certingly were a-toastin' muffins 'ot and 'ot for us, thro' me a-likin' to butter 'em myself, but can't stand the toastin', cos the fire do ketch your face so ; and 'ad 'ad a muffin and a crumpet for 'er own tea, cos I can't a-bear eatin' everything up yourself, and not a-thinkin' of a ser-vant, as is flesh and blood arter all said and done. I think Miss Brayim were of Ebru distraction 'erself, a-judgin' by the nose, and bein' that corpilent, as she says is only four-and-twenty, tho' the figger of forty, and let out as 'er aunt were married to old Jacobs in the second'and line, as is one of the children of Israel, as the sayin' is, as all looks Jewy. Not as I'm one to throw anyone's religion in their face, and 'ave seen Miss Brayim eat 'am as free as Mr. Spurgin, as I've 'eard say glories in a pork chop, as he calls 'is Christshun privileges." So Brown, he says, " I'm sure I don't want you to set with no servant gals, and would rather as you'd set quiet 'ere and keep awake, so as to 'ear wot's a-goin' on in the world."

"Oh!" I says, "I knows the time of day, and tho' I may look like a fool, I'm up to a thing or two, as the sayin' is, and wasn't a-goin' to be took in by that there Californian gold chain as Miss Brayim wanted me to 'ave for thirty shillins, as she said were worth five pounds by the weight alone."

As I says to er, " I'm sure I don't want to wear five pounds round my neck, as would sink me like a shot, if upset in a boat, as I was once when a gal in Chelsea Reach, and went down twice, as the third time would 'ave been my end, only Charley Mansfield took and 'it me over the 'ead with the boat-'ook, as he were a-tryin' to 'itch me out with, as stunned me, so then in course I come to the top and floated, thro' bein' a dead weight, as water will always give up, jest like a dead dog, as always turns with the tide, and so floats back'ards and for'ards for days, as I've seen 'em myself scores of times jest agin Battersea Bridge, as would cling to the piles."

Says Brown, " When you've quite done goin' on about Jews and dead dogs and all manner like that, preaps you'll listen, cos ere's somethink as you might like to know."

I says, " Wot's that."

" Why," he says, "Gladstin, he's reglar floored, and the Queen 'ave been and sent for Disreely."

" Well," I says, " for my part, I think it's six o

one and 'arf a dozen of the other, as the sayin' is;
and we shall have to pay just the same; but I must
say as I am glad as Gladstin is floored, cos the way
as he were a-interferin' with parties over their beer,
and then a-sendin' fellers to ask 'ow many children
you'd got, and where they went to school, as is wot
I consider a-pryin' into families, as there's a many
as wouldn't care to be asked sich questions, as give
poor Mary Ann Blinks that shock as brought on a fit on
the door-mat afore she could answer the question."

As she certingly were the plainest 'eaded one
I ever see, and no figure to speak on, not as that
were any excuse for that tally man a be'avin' as he
did to 'er a-comin' reglar every Toosday for to col-
lect the money and gettin' a good lunch, leastways
a snack, and 'is pint of bitter, and at the end of
eighteen months to tell 'er as he were a married
man and father of five already.

Not as Mr. Gladstin could 'ave knowed that,
cos in course he's a man arter all, and wouldn't go
to 'urt any 'ooman's feelin's, tho' she might be
blear-eyed in the name of Blinks, as the feller as
come round about her children thought were Mrs.
Wandel as keeps the 'ouse with a brass plate on the
door thro' Wandel bein' in the coal trade once, and
tho' dead many years she could never bear to 'ave
their fam'ly pride took down, in a-givin' up the
plate, as certingly were a noble bit of brass, tho'

the black in the letters is nearly all rubbed out, as
were thro 'usin' vitriol to it too frequent, as is a thing
I never allow, cos I always says my coal scuttle and
kittle will always come bright enuf if greased
afore bein' put on the fire.

Says Brown, "Do you know, Martha, I shouldn't
wonder but wot we shall see great changes."

"Ah!" I says, "I shouldn't wonder, cos," I
says, "wot 'as been may be, as we all knows, and I
am sure the changes as I've see myself as aint sixty
yet, would make my dear mother stare, and wot
must parties see as lives to ninety, for there is old
Mrs. Codlinton as is over ninety, she can't 'ardly
believe 'er senses, as 'ave got 'em all but her teeth
and 'air, as is both false, and when I told 'er as
they was a-goin' to take down Northumberland
House, busted into tears, and says, 'I do 'ope as the
Lion won't come to want.' For she were born in
Chandos Street, poor thing, as 'er father kep' a
brush shop, two doors off my own grandfather, and
was friends to my dear mother's dying day, and five
years older for that matter, and were born the year
of the riots, and 'ad a uncle as were shot behind Temple Bar a-tryin' to get thro' with the
Lord Mare a-chargin' the rioters right and left, as
made King George larf till he cried when they told
'im about it, and all as he could keep on sayin' was,
'I 'ope as you peppered 'em,' as went to St. Paul's for

to return thanks for gettin' of his reason back agin, as wasn't much to be thankful about, for he never had much, and very soon lost that as some say thro' ill-usage, as couldn't a-bear 'is eldest son to be a-rulin' while he was alive, as was called Prince Regent arter Regent Street and the Regency Park."

Brown, he kep on a-readin' to me bits as I likes to 'ear 'im, cos 'is remarks is that sensible over everythink, and he says, " Martha, in my opinion, you'll see as Disreely will take and do things as Gladstin didn't dare to."

"Well," I says, " he may do as he pleases, so as he don't interfere in no family matters, and don't tamper with the beer."

Says Brown, " If he's 'arf sharp he'll take and put the saddle on the right 'orse, and make the rich pay the taxes, and lighten the poor man's load, that's wot he'll do. Cos," he says, " it'll come better for the swells to give up somethink of their own accord, than 'ave it took from 'em by a lot of roughs, as'll come into power if Disreely can't govern the country."

I says, " We don't want nobody to govern the country as long as Queen Wictorier lives, bless 'er; and I knows if I was 'er, I'd take things a deal more into my own 'ands, and not let a lot of fellers do as they please, cos people would take things better from 'er, if she was to say straight out as she

wished it; but in course don't like to 'ear them
ministers a-sayin' as it's 'er Majesty's pleasure for
to 'ave this, when it ain't no pleasure to 'er at all,
any more than a-keepin' anyone in prisin durin' 'er
Majesty's pleasure, as is the reason, I suppose, as
they've let so many out lately, cos it's many a long
day since 'er Majesty took any pleasure in anythink, poor dear soul; tho' it's a pity as she 'aven't
'ad somebody to rouse 'er up, like the old Dook of
Wellington, as would be pretty nigh as old as Jeru-
salem, as the sayin' is, if livin', but yet could 'ave
put in a word, and not much over a 'undred neither;
cos 'im and Bonyparty was born the same day as I
can remember werry well 'im a-dyin' over there in
a tremendous thunder-storm, tho' quite a child, as
I've see a picter on 'im a-standin' under a willer
tree, as is werry dangerous in a storm, and would
rather get soaked thro' and thro' myself afore I'd
put up my umbreller, as might act as the conductor
to the lightnin'; and bring the lectric fluid down
the 'andle; as in course would run into the 'and
and up the 'arm to the 'art; if you 'appened to be
left-'anded, or even a-usin' of it to rest your right;
as I'm sure I've done scores of times myself, thro'
them alpackers bein' such a weight when wet, as
makes me often think of my gingham, as were
carried out to sea, with a sigh, off the cliffs at
Margate."

"But," I says to Brown, "don't you think as Gladstin will turn on Disreely when he meets 'im like a basted bull."

"Oh! yes," says Brown, "Dizzy must look out as he don't make a false step, or he'll 'ave 'is 'eels tripped up, and down he'll go."

"Ah!" I says, "and a nasty fall he'll get on them polished floors, partikler at 'is time of life, as is a-gettin' on like the rest on us." I says, "I'm glad I ain't Catherine Gladstin as rites about all the good she's a-doin' in the papers, as'll 'ave a nice job to keep 'im sweet, now he's at 'ome all day, I should say; as must feel 'is fall werry much, arter a-doin' all as she could for to please the ruffs, and come out a-bowin' and a-smilin' that sweet at 'er own winder, poor thing, and rode in a waggin' to Black'eath, as I considers werry noble on 'er, jest to purtect 'er 'usban' from dead cats and cabbidge stumps, as he'd 'ave got throwed at 'im pretty free if he 'adn't the presence of mind for to take his wife and dorter along with 'im."

Not as ever I shall ever respect 'im no more arter 'im a-singin' them infidel praises afore a mob, cos tho' he mayn't be no religion 'isself no longer, yet he didn't ought for to brag on it in public like that, as is a-settin' a bad esample, as is wot I don't consider as nobody didn't ought to do, for I've knowed parties myself as 'adn't no more religion

than cocks and hens, as walks about while other people
goes to church, yet sent the children to church,
and would go theirselves now and then, partikler in
new clothes, jest for the look of the thing, and
remembers one Lord Mare as were a Jew a-goin'
to St. Paul's in that state as he were called to, and
set and listened to a bishop a-preachin', tho' in
course he were a-larfin' in 'is sleeves, as the sayin'
is, all the time. Cos in course that bishop were
a-doin' of 'is dooty in tryin' to conwert 'im all the
time, and in my opinion it's a pity as they don't
make a Jew a archbishop, that would be the way to
conwert 'im, cos then he'd see what a 'appy thing
it is to be a good Christshun; and live in a pallis
and give up the world, with 'is wife and family;
cos if that ain't Christianity wot is I should like to
know.   And it wouldn't go agin a Jew's conshence
to be made a archbishop, as it does agin a Christshun's, as not one on 'em would do it if it wasn't as
Queen Wictorier will make 'em, and could send 'em
to the Tower if they was to refuse, jest as that old
hangel Queen Lizzybeth did used to, a-usin' sich
frightful langwidge to 'em as terrified them poor
old gentlemen to death; so they let 'er 'ave 'er
own way, and that's 'ow it is as she come to be
'ead of the Church, the same as Queen Wictorier is to
this werry day, but too much the lady to swear at a
bishop, and threaten with a hoath to strip 'is black

sattin frock off 'im with 'er own 'ands, as wouldn't
leave 'im nothink but 'is gaiters and 'is apron to
stand upright in, poor man; as wouldn't be a-treatin' 'im with respect, in my opinion.

Says Brown to me, "They'll soon make Gladstin's five millions fly."

I says, "And so much the better; wot do we
want with savin'? for wot we wants is the money
spent, why, wotever is savin' five millions, and then
go and pay those Yankee doodles three millions
down under false pretences as were a mean transac-
tion, as they deserves to be turned out for. Cos
they wos either tryin' to cheat the Merrykins when
at first they refused to pay, or else they let them
arterwards cheat us through being afraid on 'em."

Says Brown, "I'm sure nobody in this world can't
want war, but we shall be drove to give the Merrykins a good 'idin' some day, jest to teach 'em as they
didn't ought to let theirselves be ruled over by a set
of tinkers and tailors as they are, and then the Mer-
rykin gentlemen would take and rule the country
proper instead of leavin' it all to a set of thievin'
roughs, as ain't got neither manners nor yet morals.
Cos I considers Merrykins jest like our Westry 'as
none of the respectable parties in the parish will be
seen in; and so it is as things is all mismanaged
by a ignorant lot as grinds down the poor so as to
get the pickin's for theirselves."

I says, "Right you are, Brown, as speaks like
a book, as the sayin' is;" and I'm sure I often
thinks it's a pity as Brown ain't in Parlyment, or
somewhere as he could be 'eard, for he's a man as
'ave got things in 'is 'ead as never 'ardly comes out,
as if they did would make parties open their eyes,
as the sayin' is.

Brown kep' on readin' bits to me, as certiugly
did set me a-wonderin' wotever he meant about
Gladstin's surplus, as I says, "How come he to
have a surplus as ain't a clergyman?" and well I
remembers when fust they took to preachin' in
'em the row there was in a church down somewhere in the East, as were poor Mrs. Pantler's
church, as she never missed twice of a Sunday
tho' only the frce seat, jest opposite the Commun-
ion, as she set a-facin' of twenty-two year, and
told me 'erself where she see the minister walk out
on it with a couple of candlesticks and go up in the
pulpit without a-changin' 'is black gownd she
thought she should have dropped, and went 'ome a-
sobbin', and never entered a church agin to 'er
dyin' day, as were over twelve year, but read 'er
lessons and 'ole duty of man at 'ome, but said as she
never could set and see Popery, as she considered
candlesticks and a surplus afore 'er very eyes, tho'
she believed as the minister meant well, poor man,
and didn't 'old with them riots in the church, as

made 'im give in at last, cos in course the churchwar-
dens knowed wot wos right to be done in church
better than 'im, and stopped the Church Rate, and
the pew-rents dropped to nothink, so in course he
couldn't live on 'is surplus, and so chucked up the
lot, snuffed out 'is candles, and went back to 'is black
gownd, and lived 'appy ever arter, as the sayin' is,
tho' the people wouldn't never forgive 'im for tryin'
of it on, and 'ad a empty church all to 'isself.

Brown says, " I do wish as you'd ask wot is
meant by words as you don't understand the meanin'
on, and not go a-gallopin' off with the bit atween
your teeth."

" Well," I says, " I should like to get a bit
atween my teeth now for I'm quite peckish, and it's
rabbits and onions as we've got for supper, and I
thinks as old Dizzy'll keep till we've polished them
off, and I don't want my supper spilte not for all the
politics in this world ; cos as I said before, I don't
much care who is in and who is out, and so I told
Mr. Joblins as were in the licensed wittlers' line, 'as
'ave swore wengeance agin Gladstin and his lot over
and over agin in my 'earin' ; and 'is words 'ave
proved true, and I do believe as that man is a profit,
for he said as the Rising Sun wouldn't never last,
and as the Half-Moon would get on, and true his
words proved."

Brown, he couldn't hardly put 'is paper down not

to eat 'is supper, and even then didn't seem to relish
it thro' bein' so full of the general election as were
a-comin' on ; but he certingly did eat his rabbit
with a bit of toasted cheese to foller, and when
he got his pipe and drop of grog arter it, he
set there like a king still a-gloatin' over 'is
paper.

"Well," I says, "there's one thing as I'm glad
on."

Says Brown, "Wot's that?"

"Why," I says, "it must be the end of the
Tichbung trial, cos," I says, "the judge and jury
can't set a-wastin' their time over that rubbish when
they might be wanted elsewheres, cos in course
Queen Wictorier will want all the best judges round
'er for to take 'er pick of 'em to be ministers."

Says Brown, quite sharp, "Oh! rubbish."

"Well," I says, "it may be 'rubbish' is a
casy word to use, but 'ow about the jury? Suppose one or two on 'em was to go into Parlyment, they could set there till the day of judg-
ment a-listenin' to that there Chief Justiss as may
go on a-talkin' till the last day, tho' they do say he's
a-gettin' werry near the end, as must be a wonderful
long-winded party to set there a-talkin' a 'orse's 'ind-
leg off, as the sayin' is, not as I've read it, cos my
mind were made up, as the sayin' is, long ago, as
nothink won't ever make me change thro' bein' a

mother myself, and I know werry well wot I should
'ave done if Joe'd been lost at sea and come 'omo
arter twelve year and never come to see me, and
then took me up a lot of stairs to find 'im in bed
with 'is clothes on, with only the baçk of his head
turned to me. I know as I should 'ave took and
throwed my arms round 'is neck pretty tight, cos
nothing ain't stronger than a mother's feelin's, and
I'd 'ave made 'im feel as I were his mother all over."

Brown, he looks up at me and says, "'Ave you
made out wot a surplus is?"

I says, "In course I 'ave, as is a minister white
gownd, in course."

"No," he says, "it's wot a minister 'got over and
above wot he's spent, and it's five millions."

"Well, then," I says, "by the time as they'vo
been and paid for this 'ere Shanty war and sent tho
money for to feed them other niggers as is starvin'
over in Ingee, our surplus 'll look werry like a 'aporth
of soap arter a 'ard day's wash, as the saying is."

"Oh!" says Brown, "Coffee 'll 'ave to pay for
that war."

"What," I says, "put a tax on coffee, as is roso
in price already?"

Says Brown, "It ain't no use talkin' to you,
old gal, arter supper, cos then all as you're fit for is
your bed."

I says, "I'm not a-goin' till my feet is warm,

and please the pigs, as the sayin' is, I'll put a sand
bag at the bottom of that door to-morrer, for there's
a draft as comes under it enuf to cut your feet off
like a knife."

Says Brown, " 'Ave a teaspoonful more 'ot."

I says, " If I do, I'll take it up with me, for I
feels as if I'd got a weight at my chest."

"Well," says Brown, "I think you might
espect that arter the supper as you've put away,
and I do 'ope you won't get a-dreamin' that 'eavy
for your snores is like a steam-ingin a-puffin'."

"Ah!" I says, "that's when I lays too much
on one side, so if I disturbs you, take and roll me
over gentle, that's a dear."

He says, "Roll you over indeed, I should like
to see any one as could do it."

"Well," I says, " any one might, for I'm that
light sleeper, as if you was to whisper in my ear
you'd wake me."

"Ah!" he says, "I dare say if I got a speakin'-
trumpet 'andy."

I must say as I felt 'urt at Brown's remarks,
cos I am a light sleeper, as many 'ave told me, as
I've set up with, but it ain't no use a-arguin' with
Brown, so while I was a-givin' my feet a warm,
he took and read to me all about Gladstin's lot
a-goin' to Windsor for to fetch away their things,
and bein' jeered at by the wulgar crowd, as was

already for to bow down afore Disreely, as come to
'is new place all smiles and curls, not as it were
new, cos he's 'ad it afore, and knows Queen
Wictorier's ways, and where to find things, so it
ain't like 'avin' strangers for 'er ; as if she's like me
she can't abear, and I'd put up with a deal from a
servant as knows my ways, rather than change.

No doubt that Gladstin knowed that, and that's
why he took so much on 'isself, a-orderin' this
thing, and a-changin' that, and showin' 'is temper, all
over the place. As to Lowe, I never could abear
them fair men, and don't like even a white cat with
pink eyes, as is in general deaf; and then there was
Airtin, as nobody couldn't abide ; and that there
Dook of Argyle, he give 'imself them airs as is
werry well for Injier, but won't do for Ingland, and
tho' is son 'ave married Queen Wictorier's own
dorter, that don't make 'im a royal family.

So I think it's as well as Queen Wictorier 'ave
sacked the lot, cos if she'd 'ave kept one, he'd 'ave
set the others by the ears, as the sayin' is ; and
now these 'ere new uns will 'ave a fresh start, and
no follerers allowed; tho' I suppose them Duchesses
is allowed to 'ave their 'usbands come, and see 'em
downstairs, tho' it must be werry unpleasant, jest
as my Lord Dook is a-settin' over 'is cup of tea
with 'is good lady, for 'er to 'ave to jump up and
go to anser the Queen's bell, as is too much the lady

to disturb 'em at their meals, but must ring for wot she wants, as might be coals, or a glass of water, or a clean 'ankercher, as nobody under a lord durst take the liberty to 'and to 'er, and then only on 'is bended knees, in shorts, with a sword on and powder, I've 'eard say.

Brown says, " Don't stop up for me, Martha, you go to bed, for I wants to give a eye to this 'ere summin' up, as is over, but I shan't read it all."

I says, " For mussy sake don't, for," I says, "I do believe I could sum it up in 'arf a dozen words myself." So up I goes and gets into bed, for bless your 'art, I knowed 'ow it would be, as Brown would keep on a-readin' and a-readin', and I'd been a-droppin' off asleep, ever so long afore he come up, and I could 'ear 'im a-mutterin' " wonderful man," and " what a memory," and all like that ; illudin', no doubt, to that there Chief Justiss, as certingly must be fond of that there Tichbung, to set there day after day a-gloatin' over 'im ; and 'ow he can do it I can't think, as must 'ave got 'is settin' unmentionables on, as the sayin' is, with the gift of the gab into the bargain, as should 'ave give 'im a lifer myself years ago, a lyin' scoundrel, and as to one of the jury a-'oldin' out, I don't believe as there's a 'onest man out of a madhouse in all Ingland as don't look on that corpilent wiper as a foul-mouthed reptile, as the sayin' is ; and ought to be crushed like a

serpint under your 'eel, as crosses your path. But
thank goodness, it will soon be over, not but wot
I've give it up myself this many a day; and so 'ave
Queen Wictorier and the rest of the royal family, no
doubt; and as to your a-sayin' as I'm a-snorin',
Brown, 'owever can I be, when I ain't been reglar
asleep yet, only layin' ere a-ruminatin' like a lamb
at 'is mother's breast, thro' a-thinkin' of many
things, with this ere war agin the niggers, and
Gladstin and Dizzy a-crossin' of my mind, and I'm
sure I feels for Queen Wictorier, as must lay 'er
royal nightcap on many a-uneasy pillar, a-thinkin'
over what's a-comin' in the mornin' thro' the tele-
graft, as pre'aps might be war broke out with
the Roosbins, or massacree of Wolly, or the fall
of Baberlon, or the end of everythink by Dr.
Cummin come true; and I'm sure Brown needn't
talk of snorin', for 'is was more like growls of
distant thunder a-rumblin', and that's why I'm
sure I weren't asleep, when I see Disreely come
a-floatin' like a sperrit thro' my room with a smile
on 'is lips, as set down as light as a feather on the
foot of our bed, and says, "Escuse me, Martha, but
my 'art's that light as I 'ope you don't feel my
weight on your feet."

I says, "You never was a man of no weight in
my opinion, tho' a wonderful 'and at chaff." "'Ear,
'ear," says a woice, and if there didn't set Queen

Wictorier in 'er crown and spectre, a-lookin' that solim, and then I see as she were a-settin' in 'er Cabinet Counsil.

I says, "Escuse me, your grashus, but I can't think 'owever I got in 'ere, as was in my own bed a minit ago," and jest then I 'eard a snortin' snore as made me jump, and there were old Gladstin with 'is 'ead back and 'is mouth opin, as fast as a church, as the sayin' is.

I were a-goin' to give 'im a drive in the side for to wake 'im up, when Old Dizzy says with a grin, "Let 'im sleep, we shan't want 'im, shall we, your grashus, for some time to come, and then only to turn 'im out agin."

"Not a-knowin' cannot say," says Queen Wictorier, with a solim bend, as were a snub for Dizzy, leastways, I see 'im pull 'isself up.

"So," I says, "I think he did ought to be woke up, if it's only to ask 'im wot busyness he 'ad a-sendin' our brave sojers to be massacreed by them black beast."

"Ya! ya! ya!" says a woice, and there set King Coffee in a white 'at, with his umbreller up, and ridiculous shirt collars, a-playin' with 'is bones.

"You shet up," says Dizzy, a-glarin' at 'im, "and don't speak afore your betters."

"Yes," I says, "and 'ow about them ounces of gold as you promised to pay us?"

He only gave a chuckle like, and says "Golly, golly, golly, me 'umbug old Woolsey Poolsey, me no pay, but ketch 'im nice in a trap."

I says, "You good for nothink, lyin', black beast; why, your as bad as Ortin;" when up comes Wolly all of a bustle, and says "He's a friend of mine, I won't see 'im put upon," and he ketches off 'is white 'at, and takes up a banjo and begun a-singin'

I says "Drat your noise."

Says the Lord Chief Justiss, a-lookin' over the foot of the bed, "I can't 'ave this row, so you please get out."

"I'm only in the well," says Wolly.

"Let well alone," says the Lord Chief, "cos I'm sure that ain't no place for you, as is where truth lies."

He says, "I never told no lies."

Says the Claimint a-wakin' up with a snort, "No, you never did, and wot the noble judge says is true, cos it's truth as lies."

"Don't address the court without your wig and gownd on," says Queen Wictorier, a-lookin' that stern, up by the side of the judge as made that there 'og in harness trimble in every limb.

I says, "Right you are to make 'em stick to them things, for," I says, "your Majesty don't know the way as parties is a-goin' on jest like Merryker,

where the judges is just like common people, and
'ave see 'em myself a-chewin' the cud like beasts
of the field, as the sayin' is."

Up jumps Gladstin, with sich a yawn, as made
me say, " Do put your 'and afore your mouth, for I
can see down your throat."

He says, " Who's been a-sayin' as it's my fault
as them blacks 'ave been and very near licked us ? "

Says Queen Wictorier, a-lookin' werry stern,
" Didn't you say as there was lots of rice for 'em
all, and now they're a-starvin' by millions, and ain't
I cut off rice puddin's from my own royal table, as
is things as we're all partial to thro' 'avin' brought
up my royal family on 'em, as roast leg of mutton
and a baked rice puddin' were a standin' dish, and
'ave 'ad the Prince of Wales put in the corner over
and over agin for a-darin' to leave it, and made
Alfred say 'is Kattykism back'ards, for a-darin' to
call it beastly."

" Ah ! " I says, " you 'ave brought 'em up
well, you have," I says, " tho' I considers as the
Kattykism straight thro' is a puzzler for a child,
and must be werry confusin' back'ards."

" What is your name ? " says Dizzy, a-turnin'
on me sudden like, it's a mussy as I remembered
for to answer M or N, for we was in Westminster
Abbey, as were all werry grand with picters and
candles, as were bein' got ready for this ere

Rooshin Princess, and there were a party a fallin'
down and kissin' of a picter. I says to the werger
as were a-showin' us round, " Whoever is he ? "

" Oh ! " he says, " our dean, as is pertendin' to
believe the Rooshin religion, jest to please this
ere Grand Duchess, as don't believe in our ' Dearly
Beloved,' cos he's a reg'lar freethinker, and don't
believe in nothink partikler, and 'ates the Pope
with all 'is 'art."

" Well, he's paid to do that," says I, " and it's
werry nat'ral as he should, cos he knows werry well
as the Pope would soon give 'im the sack, if he 'ad
'is way, cos he don't allow no freethinkers in 'is
church, and quite right too. Cos wotever is the
use of stickin' up a church and then lettin' every-
one believe jest wot they likes, cos they can do that
without no church."

Says Dizzy, " I'm the head of the church."

" You be blowed," says a party in large musling
sleeves.

"Oh ! oh ! " says Dizzy, a-winkin' at me,
" that's your little game, is it ? My Lord Bishop,
you jest wait till either of them archbishops drops,
and see what I'll do."

" Hold your row, can't you," says some one,
" we're in conwocation. " Turn that old woman
out," says a party in a shovel 'at.

" Let 'er stop, George Antony," says another;

"she'll only make one old woman more. You're a profane person, Arthur," says another, and he certingly were, for all the time as them old swells was a-talkin', that there Arthur kep' on a-larfin', and jeerin', and winkin'.

"Well," I says, "I don't consider this be-'aviour for a place of worship."

Says that there Dean to me in a whisper, "It's all tomfoolery; we're only 'avin' a lark, and goin' to make John Bright a bishop, jest to send 'im to the 'Ouse of Lords, cos he's sich a reg'lar old square toes, and stops the way."

"Ah!" I says, "them 'umble parties like Quakers is jest the ones for bishops."

"'Umble, be blowed," says Dizzy, "I won't 'ave it; the only 'umble people is the 'Ebrer race."

"Oh! indeed," I says, "then why not make a Jew a bishop, as I said afore."

He says, "You wait a bit, and see what I'll do."

"Well," I says, "go on, only don't go too far, cos tho' you've got in, your turn to be dissolved may come sooner than you espects."

"Yes," says Gladstin, a-puttin' out 'is tung at 'im, "and if ever I comes in agin I'll makes Bradlaw Archbishop, Onsler Chief Justiss, and Wolly Lord Chancelor, and the Claimint he shall 'ave the 'andlin' of the till, and receive all the taxes, so as he

may penshun off all 'is friends, and that's 'ow to
govern a country."

I say, "Don't go on like that, Gladstin, don't ;
for I can't get to sleep for you a-tossin' of your
arms about."

He says, "I ain't Gladstin, Martha," as I knowed
to be Brown's woice. "Why," he says, "you're
frightful restless."

I says, "And so would you be if you 'ad as
much on your mind as me, and Queen Wictorier
a-ringin' of 'er bell like mad for 'er clean things,
as is that damp I must air 'em, or she'll get 'er
royal death of cold, and I'm sure I wish as they'd
give one of them Duchesses the job of lookin' arter
'er wardrobe, for I'm downright sick on it, and
can't get the things 'ome from the mangle, tho' the
gals been for 'em twice, as I believe is all Gladstin's
spite, as won't turn it for 'is wife, poor soul, cos
he's lost 'is place and 'ave gone dead sulky, and
wouldn't go down to Winsor not to say I wish you
a good mornin' to Queen Wictorier, as 'ave been a
good missis to 'im."

Says the Prince of Wales, "Oh! Mrs. Brown,
would you mind a-sewin' a button on for me, for,"
he says, "I ain't got another shirt, for they couldn't
wash nothink for me in Roosher cos it ain't the
custom of the country."

I says, "In course not, my dear boy, for 'ow

can they with the place all froze up, as would
'ave to send 'undred of miles to borrer a pail of
water."

Says a woice in my ear, "Are you goin' to bring
my——"

I knowed it were Queen Wictorier's a-callin'
over the bannisters for 'er clean things, and if they
wasn't gone, jest while I turned round to speak to
the Prince of Wales.

I says, "I shall lose my 'ead on Tower 'Ill if
them royal things 'ave got scorched, and I were
a-lookin' for 'em all round, when I see Dizzy's curly
pole on all fours, a-lookin' about on the floor.

"Why," I says, "wot do you want?"

He says, "That feller Gladstin says as he've
give up the seals to-day, as nobody didn't see 'im
do; and must 'ave done it while Queen Wictorier
were a-readin' of the noospaper, cos they ain't to
be found 'igh nor low."

I says, "Is it a bunch? cos pre'aps Low's got
'em, as may 'ave put 'em in 'is pocket without
thinkin'."

"Walker," says Dizzy, "he's jest the party to
do anythink without a-thinkin'"

I says, "You won't find 'is match in a 'urry."

Says Gladstin, "Ah! you old women never can
forget 'im about the matches."

I says, "You're jest the feller as we wants,

where is Queen Wictorier's seals, as she trusted you with ? "

He says, " Ow about that; why I've give 'em up all right."

" Then," I says, " no doubt Queen Wictorier 'ave been and put 'em on 'er watch chain, thro' bein' that worreted."

Says Dizzy, " 'Ow can she 'ave got 'er watch on, when you're a-keepin' of 'er a-shiverin' for 'er things, as can't 'old a council all thro' you, as is a-playin' into William's 'ands, you old cat."

I says, " Why there's Queen Wictorier a-settin' 'oldin' of a court, so must 'ave got 'er things; " and so she were, and noble she looked, and the moment as she see me, beckoned for me to come to 'er, a-sayin' to me with a smile, " What a time you've been, Martha, a-comin' "

I were a-goin' to say somethink about the Prince of Wales a-wantin' of a button on, when I see 'im close to 'is Royal ma, as give me a look not to say nothink, cos I dare say it would 'ave brought on words atween 'is wife and 'er ma-in-law.

As was the cause of me a-quarrelin' with my son's wife over in Merryker, cos she neglected 'is things that shameful, and 'oles in 'is stockin's as you could put your fist thro'.

So then Queen Wictorier she says to me, " Ain't this jolly news from a shanty ? "

"Ah!" I says, "they lives in 'em over in Merryker, and it's 'igh time as they knocked the 'ouses about them black beastes ears, a-darin' for to fire on their betters; but," I says, "I knowed as Card'nal Wolsey would soon settle 'em, for he always were a great man, as I 'eard all about that day as I went to 'Ampton Court, as was built by 'im, but," I says, "I do 'ope that King Coffee won't be a-wantin' to come and stop here like the Shah."

"Oh!" says Queen Wictorier, "I don't much care 'cos old Dizzy 'll 'ave to look arter 'im, and he's never so 'appy as when he's a-dancin' and a-singin' to the banjo, so they 'll get on fust rate, and Alfred, he'll chime in with wiolin when he gets 'ome, so they can amuse theirselves, and not bother me."

"But," I says, "Dizzy 'll 'ave somethink else to do now he've come in, and mustn't be a-idlin' of 'is time with a banjo, and sich rubbish. Whyever not let Gladstin learn it, as would be somethink for 'im to do, for I'm sure 'is good lady won't want 'im at 'ome all day a-idlin' about."

"Law," says Queen Wictorier, "he's sich a temper, he'd take and pull Coffee's wool out by the 'andful, and spank 'im with the banjo afore arf a 'our was over their 'eads."

"I say 'ow he must long to get 'is fingers among

old Dizzy's curls, as would come out by the roots, no doubt."

Says Queen Wictorier, "Oh, they'll never pull together; but I don't care, and so long as they be'aves theirselves afore me, 'cos if they don't, I'll fetch 'em sich a topper with my specter as 'll wake 'em both up, 'cos I ain't a-goin' to stand no Beast-mark's ways over we, as is a reg'lar bully over that there old psalm-singin' William."

"Ah!" I says, "so I've 'eard, and I do wish as your grashus would 'ave a bit more, as is as tender as a chicken."

"Never enjoyed anythink more in my life," says she, a-layin' down 'er knife and fork, as 'adn't 'ardly touched a bit, as were biled pork and greens, as we'd got for supper, and Brown a-settin' there with 'is paper, as I wanted to give 'im a nudge, jest to say as it were Queen Wictorier, for fear as he should make a 'ole in 'is manners, as the sayin' is; not as he's one ever to speak agin 'er, nor yet the Royal Family, and always stickin' up even for that there Prince Christshun, as everybody abuses.

But jest as I were a-goin' to put my foot on 'isn I see as it weren't Brown at all, but Dizzy isself a-settin' there a-pitchin' into the pork like anythink, as shows as he's a sincere Christshun any'ow, as I were glad to see, for Brown's one as don't believe in conwerted Jews, tho' there's Palistine Place, near

Bethnal Green, as I've see with my own eyes as were built a-purpose to take 'em in, and a werry comfortable livin' some on 'em gets, poor things.

So a-seein' as Dizzy 'ad been and emptied 'is plate, I didn't like to ask 'im to 'ave any more, for fear as pork might grate on 'is ears, as the sayin' is, and in course shouldn't go to call it Ambrer beef, as I've knowed parties do as still kep' to the old clothes persuasion, and went to the sinny gog once or twice a-year, when they 'ad new 'ats on.

So I says, " Mr. Disreely, suppose we was to 'ave a glass," as the werry mention on seemed for to wake 'im up.

I says, " I ain't got no srub, as is a thing I knows as your people 'olds with, not as it's Passover time neither."

'Cos I wanted to show 'im as I were up to a thing or two about 'is religion.

So I says when 'is glass were full, now, I says, " You can speak out to me like a friend."

He says, " I looks on you as a mother, Mrs. Brown."

I says, " That is a good un. Why you're my senerer a good five year."

He only winked, 'cos he couldn't anser, thro' bein' a-drinkin' at the moment.

So I says, " Now I tell you wot it is; you'd better look out, 'cos you ain't got many friends, so don't you go a-playin' the fool; and a-thinkin' as nothink can't turn you out, 'cos it can; and I says, tho' Queen Wictorier is a-noddin', she's wide awake enuf not to stand no nonsense."

For there she sat oppersite me, as give a gentle snore like a lamb, as much as to say, "Right you are."

While I was a-speakin', if Gladstin didn't come and try and set on the hedge of Dizzy's chair, so I says, "You boys, be quiet, do; you'll 'ave the arm off the chair, it won't 'old two, I tell you."

"It's quite big enuf for two," says Gladstin, "if you wouldn't kick about so. Why, wake up with you, do; I think you're mad."

I says, "Where 'ave we got to, William, I says, for it's all dark."

"I tell you wot it is, I shall go and take lodgin's if you goes on like this, I can't get a night's rest for you."

I says, "Where am I?"

"Why," he says, "in your own bed."

I give sich a jump as reg'lar woke me up, and there was Brown, as said I'd been a-plungin' and a-talkin' and a-snorin' all the time as we'd been in bed.

"Why," I says, "it must be nearly mornin'."

"No," he says, "only jest gone twelve."

"Then," I says, "it ain't a mornin' dream as I've been 'avin', as always goes by contrairy's, but

a real live dream, and you see if we don't 'ear more
on it."

"Oh," he says, "go to sleep and be blowed to
you, and were off in a hinstant, but sleep I couldn't,
for I'd been put out dreadful that day, all thro' that
old thief of a tallyman a County Courtin' me over a
bill at 'is shop, as I never 'ad a rag on, but only
went with Mrs. Mardin like a friend, as no doubt
were 'er art to get me to go with 'er, a-pretendin'
as I were sich a judge of long cloth, as said 'er good
gentleman 'adn't never 'ad sich comfortable night-
shirts as I'd got the stuff for, tho' not a tally-shop,
as is a place as I never did 'old with, and never
would 'ave 'im a-comin' to my door every Toosday,
as is often a-payin' thro' the nose for rubbish, the
same as chargin' Mrs. Wellbit a guinea for a al-
packer umbreller, as turned inside out the fust time
as she put it up, with three ribs as come thro' a lan-
ceratin' the sides, and only got a flower-pot for it
at the door, as 'ad a girinium stuck in without no
root to it, so in course waterin' on it didn't do it no
good, nor yet red leadin' the outside of the pot, to
look nice for Sunday on the winder sell, but was as
dead as muttin, as the sayin' is, afore Saturday were
out."

I shan't never forget that Saturday night as
Brown come 'ome from 'Arrich, as he'd been at all the
week thro' them steamers, and brought 'ome some

ducks and young pork as all wanted cookin', partikler the ducks, as were that tender as they come
away from their bones with lookin' at.

They was werry nice for supper, but somehow
seemed to lay like lead on my chest, tho' in my
opinion it were the cream-cheese and reddishes, as
Brown said would disgest a helefant, with bottled
porter, and took a drop of Scotch whisky cold, tho'
not weak, and went to bed like a infant, and slep'
too; but law, the wishuns as I 'ad, as was King
Coffee, a nasty black beast, and the Hemperor of
Roosher a-quarrelin' over a mishunary; and then
come that Ortin, as took and set down with a flop
in my easy chair, as I'd left my work a-layin' on,
and jumped up agin' a bloated beast, as proved as
he'd got feelin's when anythink come 'ome to 'im;
and up I woke, and couldn't get off for a-thinkin'
of all manner, till I see Gladstin with 'is throat
tied up in a old worsted stockin', as I knowed meant
'is glans down, or somethink wuss.

So I says, "You'll escuse me, but in my opinion
change of hair is the best thing for you."

"Oh, bother change of hair!" says he. "Why,
ain't I jest been to the country."

"Yes," says Queen Wictorier, as were a-standin'
at 'is elber, "but, my people's Willyim, you went
too soon; but law bless me!" she says, "I can't
stop talkin' 'ere, for I've got to get to Gravesend

for to meet the young couple ; and which is the best way, rail or boat, should you say, Mrs. Brown ? "

"Well," I says, "I considers it full early for the boat ; but in course it depends on the tide."

"Ah ! " she says, " that's where it is ; and I'm so tied by the leg, as the sayin is, with them dratted Ministers and their counsels, two in one day, as is only a form as they will stand on a-fidgettin' "

"Ah ! " I says, "and a nice crack of the 'ead young Waters got thro' not a-standin' still on it, when put there thro' not a-learnin 'is lessons, and went over back'ards ;" and then I looked up, and there stood Gladstin on one form, and Dizzy on another, a-'oldin' of their books, and there set Queen Wictorier, a-lookin' the schoolmissis all over, as says, "As to you, Master G., the way as you've been and neglected all your lessons is a disgrace ; and now to want to be escused cos you'll do a sum all right next time ; why, it won't wash."

Dizzy bust out a-larfin' at them words, as made Gladstin that shirty, as seein' as Queen Wictorier were a-lookin' in 'er work-box for somethink, he took and shied 'is book at Dizzy, as ducked 'is 'ead suddin ; and if the book didn't take and 'it the Dook of Edinburrer in the heye jest as he were a-comin' in with Alexsandrowner on 'is arm, as lost 'is temper, and give Dizzy such a kick as lost 'is balance, and so did Gladstin, and over both went with sich a crash as woke Queen Wictorier up, as were noddin' over 'er work, as was darnin' stockins.

"Wot the devil's that?" says a woice, as were Brown a-settin' up in bed.

"Law," I says, "I took you for Queen Wictorier; but in my opinion that noise is the wind, as 'ave blowed down the chimbly-board in the next room, as you'd better get up and see."

He says, "I'll see you blowed fust, and then I won't."

I felt 'urt, in course, but didn't say no more, cos Dizzy he come up to me and says, "Don't you think as I might tax chimblies?"

I says, "You'd better tax the wind at once, as well I remembers when the winder tax were in."

"Why," he says, "you remembers heverythink, and pre'aps can tell me wot is good for a carbuncle."

"Well," I says, "I 'ave 'eard as soap and miste sugar is a fine thing; but," I says, "if you've got anythink like that, don't you go a-eatin' none of them candles, nor sich Rooshin dishes, as is nothink but bile."

Says Gladstin, "Oh, let 'im alone to eat dirt, if he can get anythink by it."

"Wot are you a-callin' dirt?" says the Gran' Duchess, a-turnin' as red as a turkey-cock.

"Oh, Halfred!" she says, "'erc's insults, afore ever I've put my foot ashore;" for she was a-standin' a-leanin' on 'is harm, a-lookin' out on board a wessel for to take a sight at Ingland, tho' if she started in the dark she'd be close in shore when she got up.

I says, "I wish you'd put me ashore somewheres, for I 'ates a wessel, and can't a-bear a crowd."

"Them's my sentiments," says Queen Wictorier, close in my ear; "but," she says, "'ush! they don't know as I'm aboard, as 'ave been with 'em all the time, dressed up like a bishop; and when I gets that old Stanley over, I'll show 'im who's 'ead of the Church, a-makin' a fool of hisself in church along with them Rooshins, and their goin's on, as is werry nigh as bad as the Rityeralists."

Says Gladstin, "There's three ways of lookin' at this."

"Oh, bother!" says Queen Wictorier, "don't be a-puttin' your oar in. I've 'ad enough of your three ways, as the way out is the last as you 'ave took."

I 'eard Dizzy a-sniggerin' in 'is sleeve close behind.

So to change the subjec, I says, "'Spose we was to 'ave a little music, cos I 'ear as Allysandrowner is a fine preformer."

"You 'ear 'er on the banjo," says Halfred, as took and flourished 'is bones quite close under the Prince of Wales' nose, as said, "If you 'ave been and married a 'airess, you needn't be insultin' over it."

"Oh," says Queen Wictorier, "I 'ear 'em, I 'ear 'em. It's Lorne and 'is pipes. 'Ow kind on 'im to come, as must 'ave come by the steamer!"

Then I says, "He've picked up a good bit, if he's been a-playin' on them pipes all down the river, cos I'm sure every one aboard would 'ave give 'im a 'apenny to leave off."

"Not if 'is noble pa were a-dancin'," says Gladstin, a-turnin' up 'is nose; and there, sure enuf, were that noble Muck-all-em-more, as they calls 'im in Scotland, a-dancin' in a red waistcut, and 'is 'Ighland plad, and 'avin' of 'is fling all over the deck, a-kickin' out right and left, as made the Prince of Wales draw up 'is legs quite 'orty, and say, "Why don't he go for'ard, and make a fool of 'isself?"

"He's only a re-'ersin'," says Queen Wictorier to me in a whisper, "cos we're a-goin' to 'ave a family meetin' at Winsor, and he's to dance on the lawn afore the winders, cos Halfred won't 'ave the Scotch fiddle in the room, thro' a-playin' of the wiolin 'isself, and them musishuns is always that jealous."

"Ah!" I says, "right you are, your Majesty, for them waits 'ad a fight at the corner of our street last Christmas Eve but one, as were caused cos the man on the key-bugle blowed the wiolin out of time."

"Ah!" says Queen Wictorier, "I wish there were more 'armony."

Just then up Alfred struck with his fiddle, and there was the Hemperor of Roosher and Beastmark a-waltzin' together quite lovin', and that there old German humbug of a Hemperor a-whistlin' to 'em.

I says to Queen Wictorier, "Would your Majesty like a s'rimp to take 'ome with you for tea, cos in course you can't get 'em as fresh at Winsor as you can at Gravesend, as is their native shores."

She says, "That I should, tho' we've got redishes, but let Alfred pay for 'em, as can put 'em in 'is 'at."

I says, "My 'ankercher is quite clean, as will save the cotton bag, as they charges a penny for."

"'Ang the espense," says the Prince of Wales, a-eatin' 'em with their 'eads and tails, "let's have a quart."

"Oh! Halbert Edward," says 'is Royal ma; "'ow ever can you go on that reckless?"

"Ah!" says Dizzy, to me, "he thinks he can do anythink now I'm in."

"Well," I says, "I'm sure you ain't the party to stint 'im for anythink, as didn't ought to be outdone by 'is little brother, and if I'd my way he should have double the money."

Says Gladstin, "So he should if I was in."

"Walker," said the Prince, in an under tone, atippin' me a wink, as didn't mean nothink free, but only 'is playful ways with a old friend.

I says to him, "I'll stand by you, my boy, as always was a pet of mine, and I should like to see Old Dizzy a-darin' for to let you be cut out by any Rooshin as ever sucked a candle," so I says, " you only keep quiet till I gets a word or two with them ministers, cos in course it will come better from me than from your Royal ma."

"Oh, you do spile that boy, Mrs. Brown," says Queen Wictorier, a-shakin' of 'er finger at me, with a smile, as I see were pleased at me a-takin' of 'is part, cos as she whispers to me, "Tho' not a large family, four children, and 'arty ones too I can tell you, for they've been a-stoppin' along with me, as makes a leg o' mutton look foolish, as runs into money with things such a price, and Old Nollis! I'd rather keep 'em a week than a fortnight, as the sayin' is."

"I wonder wot's the Rooshin for, do you sleep on a feather-bed or a mattress?" she says.

"Oh!" I says, " that's easy managed, cos when you show her the bed-room you can jest give the bed a punch, and say, ' Comon vous portez vous, s'lar,' as is French for it."

Says Dizzy, "It's werry rude of you for to talk Germin, Mrs. Brown, afore me."

I says, "'Owever should I know you was a-goin' to

talk anythink, as would show your manners if you
wasn't to speak till your spoke to."

Says Queen Wictorier, "That's right, Martha,
keep 'im in 'is place."

He says, in a hundertone, like, "If she'd only
do that, I don't care what she says to me."

So I says, "Well, if you're a-goin' to speak
Germin, fire away."

"Ah, ah!" says Beastmark," let's 'ear 'im, for
Gladstin made a nice mess on it, and so did that
old fool, Johnny Russell."

"Ah! but," I says, "he always were a nin-
cumpoop."

Says Dizzy, "I should be happy to try my Germin, but really don't know only two or three words."

"Then the sooner you learns the better," says
Beastmark, a-glarin' at im, "cos very soon I shan't
allow no other language to be spoke, cos it's the
only one as the Pope don't know, and I mean to
shet 'im out in the cold."

Says Queen Wictorier, "Don't you interfere
with the Pope, nor nobody else in my 'ouse, if
you please, or else pre'aps you may find yourself on
the doorstep."

"Ah!" I says, "and with them young
Prince's boots close behind you, so you jest shet up."

"No," says Queen Wictorier, "you aint a-goin'
to bully me as if I was that poor old asmatic Will-

yim, as daren't call his soul his own;" and she says, "you ain't got no friend in Mrs. Brown, so don't try and leer at 'er."

I says, "If he was to dare to, my good gentleman would give 'im sich a 'idin' as he never had afore in 'is life."

Some one bust out a-larfin', and there stood that young Bonyparty. So I said to 'im, " Remember, my dear boy, as you're nobody, so keep your toe in your pump, as the sayin' is, and don't you be took in by them donkeys of French as comes over a flatterin' of you, as only 'opes to get somethink out of you; and don't you go a-tryin' it on to get up no row in France, cos you'll find as that there Mac Marn is a reglar Paddy Wack at 'art, and if he ketches you, he'll 'ang you, and I don't think as even Queen Wictorier could beg you off, so you be a good boy, and take care of your ma, and try and forget all that rubbish about your bein' a Prince, cos you ain't nothing of the sort, and only was a sham one, though no doubt if you was to list, and keep steady, you'd rise from the ranks, as the sayin' is; but you ain't got no rights to nothink but wot you works for 'onest, so don't be persuaded to go into no dodges, as 'ave been the ruin of all your family, as might 'ave been respectable if they 'adn't been and overstepped theirselves, as is jest wot Gladstin 'ave been and done."

Says somebody to me, as proved to be Dizzy, "If you stands a-maggin' here, you'll be too late for to get a seat."

I says, "Where?"

"Why," says the Prince of Wales, "she's a-goin' to sit by me." There he were a-eatin' pennywinkles out of 'is shacko with 'is breast pin, as Alfred had brought 'em fresh from Gravesend, but obligated to eat 'em on the sly, cos Queen Wictorier can't abear the sight on 'em; he says, "Not room for Mrs. Brown! why, she should set on my knee fust."

I says "Go along with you, do; why, I should smother you with this ere jacket on."

Says the Prince of Wales, "All right, old gal, you shall 'ave Lorne's place."

I says, "Certingly not, as is your brother-in-law, and didn't ought to be turned out of 'is place; nor yet kep out of a room nowheres, not if 'is wife's there; and I do 'ope I shan't 'ear no more about them goin's on, as don't look well in families, and that's why I never will 'ave friends without a-askin' Joe Barnes, as married our Mary Ann, tho' I don't like a bone in 'is body, thro' always a-mistrustin' any one that squints backards, as can't look you straight in the face."

Says a woice, "Martha Brown, is this wot you calls a-comin' to spend the day with me on the quiet," and there I see Queen Wictorier in 'er spectacles, a-settin' at a table as were covered with work.

I says, "I were only a-sayin' a few words to them young fellers of yourn, as is so full of their fun."

"Ah!" she says, "they're like the young bears, all their troubles to come."

I says, "'Ush, there's that Ailysandrowner a-listenin'"

"Law!" she says, "she don't understand nothink."

I says, "I'm sure as she cort the word bears; as she knows is Inglish for Rooshins."

Says Queen Wictorier, a-takin' up a sock, "Now, Mrs. Brown, is this worth mendin'."

I says, "I should say not, thro' the 'eel bein' cut thro' as ain't good enuf for to graft."

She says, "Ah! that's wot I says, and it's all thro' Leopold a-bein' at Oxford, as will wear them Oxford shoes."

"Ah!" I says, "they're nasty things for to cut your socks thro' at the 'eel, but," I says, "socks ain't nothink at Oxford to wot they are at Etin, where I've 'eard of a boy as run up a bill as come to pounds for socks alone."

"Ah!" says Queen Wictorier, "I sometimes thinks who would be a mother."

"Why," I says, "you would, and proud of

them boys you are, tho' they 'ave, no doubt, give
trouble; for I could see 'er smilin', tho' she did look
grave like, when Leopold begun a-chaffin' Arthur
about bein' spoons over in Denmark.

I could see as Queen Wictorier were a-longin' to
talk to me, cos in course, poor dear, she must be
lonesome like, without a friend in the world, as no
king or queen can't 'ave, for she give a sigh, and
says, " It's awful dull work for me, Martha, but,"
she says, a-turnin' on Dizzy, as were a-puttin' on
coals in 'is new livery, as in my opinion 'ad only
been altered with new buttons, cos he looked so
like Gladstin behind, as made Queen Wictorier say,
" Uart, I would say Benjymin, mind, I ain't at
'ome to nobody."

" Please your grashus, Prince Beastmark's a-
waitin', I ve kep 'im quiet with some broken wittles
and small beer, but he says he won't go till he's
seen you."

" Won't he ? " says I, " then jest let me settle
'is 'ash," so I turns and sees 'im a-cleanin' out 'is
pipe, and says to 'im, " well, my Prooshin blue,
wot's up with you. Ah ! " I says, " you needn't
try to 'ide that bundle in your 'at, cos I knows wot
it is, it's some of the cold meat as you've been and
grabbed, and tied up in your 'andkercher."

He didn't anser, for he'd been and crammed 'is
mouth that full thro' a-thinkin' it were Queen Wic-

torier a-comin' out, and stared to see me with a crown on.

So I says "'Ow's Willyim's corf;" and tips 'im a wink to show as I knowed all about its bein' a deal wuss than wot they pertend, cos the old willin's got water on the chest, that's wot he's got, so I says, "look here, Beastmark, Queen Wictorier can't be bothered with you now, for she've got 'er 'ands full," as were true enuf, for I'd left 'er with a sock drawed over 'er left 'and, and a needle in the right.

Beastmark didn't anser, and I goes on and says, "Don't you come 'ere a-tryin' none of your games, cos you ain't a-goin' to come the bully 'ere, and if you carries it too far over there, you'll find yourself in the wrong box some day, cos that there Prince Fritz don't love a bone in your body, nor nobody else, and some fine day you'll get showed the door, and if a pistol were to go off unawares, and go thro' your 'ead, I don't think as old Willyim's 'im book would be wet thro' with 'is tears."

So jest then Dizzy come up and says, "Don't go too far, that's a good soul, Martha, cos we don't want to 'ave no row at present."

"Oh!" I says, "all right, only don't let 'im come a-cadgin' 'ere, as there's plenty of 'ungry mouths for our broken wittles, without 'im, cos," I says, "look at that Injin famine, tho' I must say as they're very foolish to live on nothink but rice, as ain't a thing to lean upon any more than a potater, as is wot the Irish sticks to; as I considers a poor substitute for the stomick to rest upon, the same as dry bread."

Says Beastmark, in a woice of thunder, as the sayin' is, " I'm blest if I stand this, I'll 'ave a pipe."

I says, " Not in my room, I 'opes."

He says, " There's a bit of fire 'ere, and I can't sleep a wink, and you're as restless as a colt."

I says, "No man but my lorful 'usband shall ever——"

He busts out a-larfin', and stirs the fire, and sure enuf he was Brown a-settin' by the fire a-loadin' of 'is pipe, as I likes 'im to 'ave when he can't sleep.

" So," I says, " glad I am as you're there, for my life's a reglar burden to me with dreams, and pre'aps the baccy will draw me off, and so it did, for I don't think as I 'ad another dream, not till I 'eard the milkman a-comin' down the street, as were a mussy, for them dreams is that 'eavy as they reglar draws me down, and the lot as you can dream in a minit or two is surprisin', for I 'eard that milkman turn the corner, and jest give myself another turn when I see Dizzy a-standin' with the kittle in 'is 'and, and givin' of Queen Wic-

torier some water in the teapot, as were at breakfast, and says to 'im, with a wink at me, "Take
care, Benjymin, as you don't burn your fingers."

So I says jest to change the subjec, "I wonders
as you don't let some of the young people make
tea."

"Oh!" she says, "Louise did use to, but I
can't trust Beetreece, she never cares whether it
biles or not; and she says I should 'ave let Ally-
sandra do it, but then there'd 'ave been jealousy,
for Allysandrowner she made it last night Rooshin
fashion, without no milk, and a slice of lemon in it
as were beastly."

"Ah!" I says, "I knows that's Rooshin ways,
cos a party as lodged with Mrs. Padwick, as knows
Roosher well thro' a travellin' in the leather line,
he showed us it, only Sunday last, and I couldn't
abear it, tho' he said it were that pure thro' a-comin'
in a carrywan, but I don't think as bein' shet up
for weeks in 'is portmanter 'ad improved it's flavour,
nor yet its colour neither."

Jest then there were a squall, and if it weren't
as Dizzy in puttin' down the kittle 'ad been and
sprinkled Gladstin's feet with it, as 'ad 'em on the
fender, for he was a-settin' afore the fire with is
'at on and 'is things in a bundle.

So I says in a whisper to Brown, I says, "
don't call that manners, keepin' 'is 'at on, but, I

says, " I suppose we must escuse 'im thro' bein' put
out, but wot's he a-waitin' for."

" Why," says Dizzy, a-chimin' in, as he's a
deal too fond on for me, he says " he's a-waitin' for
a slice off that surplus ; and don't he wish he may
get it."

I says, " Why, he can't espect you're a-goin' to
cut up a surplus for 'im ; as would be werry nigh
as bad as robbin' a church."

" Why not rob a church as well as well as anybody else ? " says Beastmark.   " I'd rob 'em all fast
enuf, only 'ere's old Willyim's got a sore throat
and funks dyin', cos he's afraid as the Pope won't
let 'im be berried like a Christshun."

" Oh ! " says Dean Stanley, as were close by,
" I'll go and berry 'im with pleasure, and in Westminster Abbey, as is where King Coffee lies too,
as is to be brought 'ome at once, salted down."

I says, " And werry disgustin' too, a-treatin' a
'uman bein' like pork. Whyever not berry 'im
where he dies ; and as to old Willyim, as he's so
pious, he can't mind dyin', and I'm sure he'll be
glad to get away from Beastmark, as won't let 'im
call 'is soul 'is own."

" Are you a-goin' to 'ave your breakfast in bed,
Mrs. Brown ? " says the Archbishop of Canterberry,
a-puttin' 'is 'ead thro' the bed-curtains.

I says, " Law, no ! I'm all right ;" and up I

jumps; and there were Brown, as said he were
goin' down to make the tea, and would I like a
round of buttered toast; so in course I got up at
once; and it wasn't till I'd 'ad two cups of tea that
I were feelin' fresh, and never got my 'ead clear
of the royal family not all that day. I'm sure I
could swear as I were wide awake that same
evenin', tho' I always do feel dosy atween the
lights, and that's why arter tea I got my work, for
fear as a book should send me to sleep, and felt as
wide awake as ever I were in my life, and the fire
a-burnin' that cheerful, and see Gladstin as plain as
a pikestaff, as the sayin' is, a-settin' oppersite to
me a-warmin' of 'is 'ands, as said he'd jest come
back from Winsor. "Ah!" I says, "no doubt
you found it cold enuf there, and I see as Queen
Wictorier wouldn't 'ave you and Dizzy set together,
or it would 'ave been 'ot enuf between you."

He says, "'Ow do you know, as wasn't there?"

I says, "Wasn't I, jest? and shan't never forget
Dizzy's face when he 'ad to drink the Hemperor of
Roosher's 'ealth in train ile."

"I wouldn't do it," says Gladstin. "I never
did eat dirt."

"Oh, didn't you, tho', old feller," says I; "'ow
about Merryker and the Hallybammer claims?
You certainly eat your full peck that time, and
made us eat it too; but," I says, "let bygones be

bygones; and now wot are you a-goin' to do for a livin', and wotever is Lowe and Airton a-goin' to turn their 'ands to?"

"Oh," says Gladstin, "they be 'anged, as was the ruin on me;" he says, "I've 'eard as Bob is a-goin' to teach rethmitic in a school; and as to Airton, Beastmark 'as give 'im a place over there, cos he wants a master of the ceremonies for to teach them Germins manners; and," he says, "as to me, I think as I'll turn commershul."

"Ah," I says, "that'll be a constant change."

Says Dizzy, in my ear, "Law bless you! my good soul, nobody won't trust 'im."

I says, "Do leave off a-aggravatin' 'im, you tiresome toad, do."

Says Queen Wictorier, a-bendin' to me out of the carridge winder, jest like I see 'er the day as she brought that there Grand Duchess into London thro' the snow, "Mrs. Brown, I 'ope they're a-takin' care of you down there, cos I can't see your plate."

I says to Brown, "Ain't it singler as Queen Wictorier should set down in 'er bonnet, with the crown on the top of it, as is wot she went in per-ceshun to the Tower for to get it out, cos in course they won't give it up to nobody but 'er own 'ands, as keeps the key of that hiron cage, as it's kep' in the Tower in, loose in 'er pocket, and not on a bunch with the rest, for fear of losin' the lot."

Says Dizzy to me, " This ain't busyness, now, Mrs. Brown; do be serous. Wot 'ave you got to say to me ? Cos Queen Wictorier 'ave told me to ask you wot I'd best take and do over this 'ere budget."

" Well," I says, " that depends."

"Ah!" says Gladstin, "my fine fellow, now you're in for it, and I wish yer joy. You'll 'ave to take off all the taxes, and put down the 'Stablished Church—not as you'll care much for that."

Says Queen Wictorier, in a woice of thunder, "I'll send you both to the block on Tower 'Ill, and you may wait there till I comes to fetch you away, if you dares me, a-skylarkin' under my nose;" and then I see as Dizzy were a-tryin' to stick a bit of paper up Gladstin's collar.

Says Dizzy, " Please, mum, I didn't go to do it, but he is that tormentin' a-makin' faces at me, and a-sayin' as I must go over to the Dissenters, and make Spurgin a bishop, as don't want it, cos he's got as much as most on 'em a'ready."

Says Gladstin, " There's three courses open tc you; one is to jine Dilke, and go in for a Republic; and the other is——"

Says the Prince of Wales, "'Old 'ard with you there. If you says that agin——"

"Do be quiet, Halbert Hedward," says the Queen;

"and let 'im 'ave 'is say, as is the British Con-stitushun."

"Yes," I says, "mam," as is wot they all calls 'er at cort; "but if he was to dare go on Black-'eath and talk about 'is three courses, he'd precious soon get 'is desserts, as the sayin' is, and serve 'im right."

Says Dilke, "I'm sure I never meant no disrespect to Queen Wictorier, as my family owes everythink to, and I ain't that ungrateful as to go and turn on my best friends; and to tell you the truth, Mrs. Brown, it's all my fun about a Republic, and I only said it jest to see wot they would all say."

"Well," I says, "my fine feller, don't you be a-playin' them larks again; cos," I says, "if you wants to see wot parties thinks on it, you'd better jest go out and say as much next time as Queen Wictorier comes thro' the streets in state, and you'll see where you'll be, with your 'at knocked over your eyes, and every rag tore off your back, before Queen Wictorier could say a word to save you."

Says Gladstin, "As I were a-sayin', there's three courses open to 'im."

"Oh!" I says, "do dry up with them three courses; for," I says, "Queen Wictorier 'ave gone to bed with 'er bonnet on; as'll give 'er a frightful 'eadache afore mornin', and no one durstn't take it off cos of the crown."

Says Dilke, " Oh ! nobody cares for the crown."

Up jumps the Dook of Edinburrer, and says, " Jest come outside, will yer, and I'll soon show yer who cares for the crown."

I says, " I'll call the perlice if there's goin' to be fightin', and," I says, " I wonders at your Royal 'Ighness a-noticin' on 'im, as no doubt could punch 'is 'ead, but might get a black eye, as wouldn't look well in uniform, and pre'aps give your good lady a turn ; so," I says, " 'ands off, and let's 'ave a round game till supper's ready, as'll be nine punctual."

Says Gladstin to Dizzy, " I'll buy your deal."

" That you won't," said Dizzy, with a grin, showin' me the Queen as he'd got, so in course only wanted a ace for to turn up a natural.

" It's my pool," says Gladstin.

" You're another," says Lowe, a-tryin' to grab the lot, and if that there Lord Shaftesbury, as were lookin' on, didn't take and pull the cloth off the table, cards and all, a-sayin' as cards was sinful, tho' two bishops was playin', but it was only 'is spite, for fear as Gladstin should win, as made Airton that wild, that he took and kicked 'is shins on the spot, as sent Lord Shaftesbury off with a 'owl, a-swearin' as he'd bring it afore Exeter 'All the very next time as Archbishop Mannin' took the chear there for a testimonial to Dr. Cummin', thro' 'im 'avin' took the pledge, and purposed the Pope's 'ealth in toast and water, when a-dinin' along with the Free-masons, as wants the Pope to be their Grand Master.

I says, "Nonsense, he don't 'old with their ways, and won't let none of 'is flocks belong to 'em, as rayther puts Brown out; not but wot he says as it's right as the Pope should 'ave 'is way, and let them as likes obey him; cos I certingly 'ave knowed some Freemasons as was 'owdashus characters, as was Mr. Bummil, the plumber and glasher, as beat 'is own wife with a sodderin' iron, and took the 'air off the crown of 'er 'ead, a place as big as a palm of your 'and, as she did used to say brought 'er to fronts at four-and-twenty, tho' I never see 'er in 'er nat'ral 'air, escept stickin' out grey under 'er cap in the nape of 'er neck, as was nearer to sixty than fifty, when we fust come to South Lambeth.   But he certingly were dreadful in 'is goin' on, and 'ad to be strapped down in bein' took to the stashun-'ouse, that time as he broke all poor Mrs. Lettlepit's winders, as lived next door, a-comin' 'ome late the wuss for licker, and a-mistakin' the 'ouse, and flew in a rage, cos they wouldn't let 'im in, when he'd been a-knockin' and ringin' 'arf a' our, as in course 'is poor wife would 'ave 'eard next door if she 'adn't been alone in the 'ouse, and could only 'ear with her left ear, as is the only side as she can sleep on, thro' bein' that asmatic as is nearest the 'art, and won't let the lungs 'ave full play if pressed on with the whole weight of the body, as in course you can't help in sleep, tho' I've knowed parties as set up in bed all night, as were a aunt of mine, and werry uncomfortable to 'ave to sleep with her, as I've done when a girl, thro' a-lettin' the cold hair down into the bed, but didn't matter so much thro' her bein' a single woman, for I'm sure it's wot Brown wouldn't never put up with, not if he'd married a Princess Royal, so no doubt the Pope is right about Freemasons, not as I believes in their secret, cos it's all my eye talkin' about a secret that is beknown to thousans, and them mostly married men. Law bless you, it's agin nature, and that's why them Rityeralists won't never get parties to be sich fools as to go a-confessin' to them, cos they knows werry well as they'd tell their wives as sure as a gun, as the sayin' is, cos in course no wife in this world wouldn't stand 'er husband keepin' a lot of things from her as he'd 'eard in the parish, as she'd be a-dyin' to know thro' 'appenin' in all the naybours' families, and a nice row there'd be. Oh! dear no, the bishops is quite right to stop such goin's on, and if they don't, why, in course Parlyment will step in and soon put it down, not but wot I should let parties do as they please, and confess to the parson and 'is wife too if they likes it, as is wot I calls liberty of conshence, as nobody

didn't ought to interfere with, nor yet rediculc, and
so I told Mrs. Pilikoo, as have joincd some of them
wild sexes, and talks of bein' converted, just as if
she'd been a Jew Israelite; but law, I ain't no time to
bother about sich things myself, and I do 'ope as
Disreely won't go a-'avin' no finger in the pie
about religion, cos he'll burn it to a certinty, and
that's 'ow Gladstin 'ave been and fell thro' a-playin'
fast and loose, as the sayin' is, with them churches,
as is all sorts and sizes—sometimes 'igh, sometimes low, sometimes broad, and sometimes no.

Says Gladstin to me in a whisper, "I'll serve 'im out,
old gal; he's got in, and I'll smoke 'im out; for if he
stops in he'll have to put down the Church, and the
Lord Mare and the City of London, with both War-
sities, and let the Hirish 'ave a king of their own, as
will pre'aps be Wolly, and sell the crown jewels to pay
the income tax, and make Ortin a judge; and I'm
a-goin' to pertend to retire, as'll only be jest round
the corner for to get a few lessons from Johnny Broome
in the noble hart of self-defence, and then see when
I've got the gloves on if I don't knock the Ebrer silly."

I says, "You'll never go a-prize-fightin'
afore Queen Wictorier's werry face, partickler
now as she've got the Hempcror of Roosher a-
drinkin' tea with 'er, and the Hempcror of Mo-
rocco expectin' to drop in to supper, cos the two on
em ain't uscd to see no sich goin's on at 'ome, and

might give you a nasty one, cos they always goes about with fire-arms, and I've 'eard say as the Hemperor of Roosher's boots is tremenjous 'eavy."

Says the policeman, as were a standin' by, " Oh ! let 'im talk, he's only a-blowin' off the steam, cos he's that wild at 'avin' made sich a fool of 'isself a-goin' and dissolvin' all of a sudden, when he might 'ave been and held together all the year any'ow, as would 'ave been a somethink in 'is pocket."

I says, " Perliceman, I'm surprised at you for to think as he'd take any tips."

He only give a wink, and then I see it were Dizzy dressed up like a perliceman, as were jist a-watchin' of Gladstin, as were tryin' to sing the Rooshin 'Imm, as they was all 'avin' a-goin' in at, with Queen Wictorier a-playin' on the pianer, and Alfred with a wiolin, and the Prince of Wales a-beatin' time, and old Dizzy, he'd got the cymbals a-bangin' away that loud, and there was Dean Stanley with a 'and organ and the pan-pipes, and 'is good lady with a tambourine, and Beastmark, he puts 'is 'ead in at the door, with his nightcap on, and roars out, " If you don't stop that there row, I'll have the lot of you run in, as must be brutes to go on like that with me, 'avin' gone to bed early and got sich a sore throat."

" Who are you callin' brutes ?" says that young Bonaparty boy, as were a-playin' with a comb and paper.

" Look 'ere," says Beastmark, " don't let me 'ave none of your cheek, young Brummygim, or else I'll give you a good thrashin', as I 'ave done your elders."

Says the Pope, " Let the boy alone, and speak civil to them musishuners, and give 'em somethink to go into another street."

Says the Prince of Wales to me, " He thinks 'isself a swell, that Beastmark does, but he'll 'ave a bad fall afore long, see if he don't, cos they all 'ates 'im, a-knowin' as 'is game is for to make 'isself fust everywhere, and only wait till old Willyim drops, and that there old Beastmark will be sold for dogsmeat."

" Law," I says, " I pities the dogs as is drove to eat 'im."

Says Queen Wictorier, " Martha Brown, ere's a present for you; it's King Coffee's umbreller, as they've been and sent me, as will be a deal more use to you than to me, thro' seldom goin' out myself when it's showery, for fear of roomatics."

" Law," I says, " what a beauty."

" Yes," says Queen Wictorier. " And I quite 'ad words with all my children 'cos I wouldn't put it up that day as I drove thro' town with this darlin' Allysandrowner."

" I'm sure," says the Princess Louise over the back of my chair, " it's a wonder as ma didn't get 'er death in all that snow, as is more than she's ever done for one of 'er own."

So I see as there was jealousy there, and says, " My dear, your ma 'ave a feelin' 'art, and in course wished to be partikler kind to this 'ere poor Rooshin young creetur, as must feel lonesome, now them crackjaw parties 'as gone back to Roosher, and left 'er."

" Oh, no, Mrs. Brown, I ain't a bit dull," says a woice, "and if it wasn't that werry Allysandrowner a-standin' by me a-feedin' of the ducks on that bit of water in the Park oppersite Buckinam Pallis."

I says, " I'm glad to 'ear it, and 'opes as the pallis ain't damp thro' bein' shet up so long, and 'ave 'eard say as all the chimblies smokes, as is why Queen Charlotte did used to take snuff, and nearly always in a bad 'umour, thro' the blacks a-settlin' all over the place, as were nat'rally a clean disposition, thro' bein' used to washin' constant, as were brought up to the clear-starchin' afore ever she thought of bein' Queen, and they do say as King George never did fancy 'er, and any time my dear, I says, as you should like to 'ear all about that old King George's Royal Family, I could tell you volumes, thro' 'avin' 'eard it all from them as knowed all about it; not as I'm no relation to the boy Jones, the young sweep as got into the Pallis thro' the chimbly, as was like 'is dirty ways, and took and listened to things as Queen Wictorier said under the sofy; as I knows a deal about myself, only in course shouldn't mention."

"If I ketches you a-sayin' a word agin Queen Wictorier, I'll jest send you to the Tower, Mrs. Brown," says a park-keeper, in a woice of thunder and a fierce glare at me."

I says, "Me say a word agin 'er, bless 'er royal 'art, never, as feels like 'er own sister, but," I says, "Mr. Dizzy, you needn't go a-dressin'-up like a park-keeper, jest to listen to wot I'm a-sayin' to this 'ere young lady, as I don't consider bein' open and aboveboard."

He didn't say nothink, but goes and pulls a boy's cap off as were a-settin' on the bank fishin' with a pin at the end of a stick and a bit of string.

"You'll leave me alone, you big bully," says the boy; and if it weren't Gladstin, poor feller, a-settin' there, jest a-tryin' to amuse 'isself, now he's out of place.

I says, "Don't be sich a spiteful old wiper, Ben, don't; it's mean on yer, and tho' Queen Wictorier, no doubt, didn't like a bone in Gladstin's body, as the sayin' is, yet I'm sure she's too much the lady to set by and see 'im put upon now, as she've been and sacked 'im."

I see old Dizzy turn pale, cos he 'adn't see as Queen Wictorier were a-settin' under a tree close by,

a-readin' of a book, with them young Waleses a-
playin' about. She weren't no more readin' than I
was, cos she got a eye on 'er grandchildren for fear
of the water, as was a-playin' werry pretty at
'orses, on a old broom, as kicked up a deal of dust,
and she were a-watchin' Dizzy too with 'er other
eye like a couple of links, as is reg'lar piercers, so
Dizzy, he pertended not to see 'er, but took and
sloped all of a 'urry, tho' pertendin' to walk slow,
a-feelin', no doubt, as he'd been and put 'is foot in
it, as the sayin' is, cos, in course, nobody don't like
to see nobody bein' kicked when they're down, as
the sayin' is."

"I wish, Mrs. Brown, as you was mistress of
my robes," says Queen Wictorier, as I were a-passin',
"for I never see a sweeter dresser, and that there
polernaise fits you like your skin."

I says, "Well, to tell your Majesty the truth,
it's a little more tighter; and cuts me dreadful
under the harms, and if I'd 'ave knowed it would
'ave turned so mild, I shouldn't 'ave wore it, but
dressed warm this mornin' cos of the snow, in goin'
to see your Majisty bring this 'ere young Duchess
into London, as will no doubt soon get used to our
ways, and must 'ave felt quite at 'ome in the snow,
as it was werry considerate for to come down 'ansom
jest then, and made 'er feel at 'ome, no doubt, and
was well ropped up, I 'ope, like the lot on you."

Jest then there was a tremendous crash, " Law,"
I says, " I 'opes as none of the little royal family,
ain't fell off that broom, and 'urt their little
royal selves nowheres, or preaps it's that Gladstin
been and broke thro' the hice, and drowned hisself,
cos he can't 'ook no more fish, or preaps riled thro'
not a-bein' able to bear to see that there Dizzy
a-standin' over Queen Wictorier, and a-tellin' 'er
wot she did she ought to say to Parlymint. So I
goes up to 'im and whispers, " You 'ad better look
out, old man, and see wot you're a-goin' to say
yourself, cos, my fine feller, every one will down on
you."

He put 'is 'and on my shoulder, and says,
" Wake up, old lady," and if I didn't look up, and
see Brown, as 'ad come in with 'is key, and fell
over the coal scuttle, as that dratted gal 'ad left in
the passage, as she said, only a minit, while she
went to turn on the gas at the metre. I jumps up
and give it 'er pretty 'ot, I can tell you, " cos," as
I says, " if you leaves anythink anywheres as is
rong, only for a minit, someone's sure to come by
at the momint, jest the same as poor Mrs. Belpitt
come to be in 'er bed for weeks, thro' a-settin'
down suddin on a lookin' glass, as 'er own dorter
'ad laid on a chair, only for a minit, as is quite enuf
for a powder magerseen to go off in under you, and
she weighed over two and twenty stun, poor soul ; as

is more than any lookin' glass in this world can be
espected to bear up agin.

So Brown he says to me, " Martha, it's werry
dangerous in you to go a-noddin' and a-blinkin'
over the fire like this."

I says, " Why, Brown, I ain't been set down
ten minits, but am that tired thro' a-standin' so
long yesterday, for to see the Gran' Duchess go by
in percession.'

" Ah ! " he says, " I thought you'd be there."

"Yes," I says, " and didn't ought to 'ave stood
at all, thro' a-payin' 'arf a crown for a werry good
place in front of a shop, as 'ad put up seats all
boarded in front, as I got a corner one, so as to see
'em well both ways. I got there all right enuf as
weren't far from the New Road, and must say it
were not a roomy seat, but bein' the front row I
didn't complain. I got into it all right enuf, and
there I set pretty nigh perished for over two 'ours,
and jest as the percession were a-comin' by, a party
settin' behind me, kept a-leanin' over on my back,
and parties behind 'er agin was a-leanin' forard
over too; and if they didn't take and shove me
right off my seat, as slipped down atween the seat
and the 'ordin in front of it, 'as 'ad been put up to
keep the crowd off, and were that jammed in, as
get up agin I couldn't; and as them boards jest
reached up to my eyes, I couldn't see nothink but

only the tops of the sojers a-ridin' by; and when they was passed I never should 'ave got out agin in this world, if they 'adn't been and knocked the boards away, for they was tight as I couldn't 'ardly get my breath. I was wexed; but must say as parties as the shop belonged to be'aved werry 'andsome, for they took me along with them by the underground, as was close by; and we got to St. Jameses Park in time to see the percession there, and then all on 'em come out on the balcony, as certingly were a sight to do your 'art good; and I didn't mind the scrougin', nor the pinchin', nor nothin' as they took out of my pocket, tho' I were sorry for my little flat bottle, as is a old friend of mine, as is things as I'm fond on, and 'ave saved my life and others' besides; so I always says, none of your teetotalin' for me, as is werry well for them as is that degraded characters as can't trust theirselves to a drain and not make beasts of theirselves, as I knowed a old feller once, as did used to boast as he'd gone to bed drunk every night for twenty years, and then took and turned teetotaler in 'is old hage, as pretty soon polished 'im off. So you see, Brown, I ain't rested yet, as no doubt, a good night will pull me thro', all straight agin."

I'd been werry much put out thro' Old Sinful agin, as 'ad rote a-warnin' the tax-gatherer, as I'd been and left our last 'ouse without a-payin' the rates, and all as we owed were 'arf a crown for gas, as were the collector's own fault; but that old wiper with one leg shorter than the other, as 'ad been a excise man, he were my bitterest enemy, all thro' me a-lettin' of 'is dorter know as he were a-goin' to marry a bit of a gal in the name of Sarah Soper, as lived there, as told our Mary Ann, over the wall, as I over'eard 'em a-talkin', thro' a bein' in the washus, a-tryin' to get some mildew marks out of a table-cloth, as must 'ave been put away damp. I didn't say a word to our gal, as I'd 'eard wot they was a-talkin' about, and shouldn't 'ave, if it 'adn't been as there were a pane of glass out of that washus winder as I'd broke myself, to let the steam thro', so I made it my busyness to say to Miss Sinful, as is ugly as a 'orse, as I met a-walkin' down the street, as orty as a Hostrich, " Good mornin', and wishes you joy of your new step-ma."

She stops short and says, " If you insults my pa any more, we'll have the law on you."

I says, " Pray do, cos insults is the last of my thoughts, and 'opes when he's married as you'll all be 'appy together."

She says, " Wot do you mean?"

" Why," I says, " you and your new stepma, Miss Soper, as is goin' to be married to your pa to-morrer morning at Spitalfields Church, and I means to be there and see."

She says, a-turnin' pale, "You don't mean it serious, Mrs. Brown?"

I says, "I ain't in the 'abit of jokin' over sich things."

She says, "Who told you?"

I says, "That's my busyness, and I wish you a good day," and on I walks, leavin' her planted like on the pavement.

Well, the next mornin', who should come in all of a hurry, jest on nine, but Miss Sinful, a-sayin', "Can I say a word to you, Mrs. Brown?"

I says, "Certingly," thro' breakfast bein' over, and Brown started, and the gal were out.

She says, "It's all true; that young 'ussey 'ave entrapped my old fool of a father into matrimony. She'd give warnin' a month ago, and left last night. I'd ketched her a-trimmin' a 'at the night afore, as she said were for 'er sister to go to a christenin' in. Well," she says, "this mornin' father were up quite early, as ain't 'is abits, nor more than me, as ain't never 'ardly down till nine, in a gen'ral way— I 'eard 'im a-movin' about in 'is room, and then I 'card 'im call; so I goes to the door, as I'd took and locked on the outside the night afore, as well as took away 'is two sticks and 'is clump, as he can't walk without. When I went in the last thing I wished 'im good-night with a basin of 'ot gruel. So when I 'eard 'im call I goes to the door, and says, 'Wot is it, father?' He says, 'Oh, is that you, Nancy? Send old Martin up to me,' as is a old feller as comes of a mornin' to do odd jobs about the 'ouse and gardin. So I says, 'He ain't 'ere.' 'Ain't he?' says he. ''Ow strange! I told 'im to be 'ere afore eight, cos I wanted 'im.' I says, ' He's been fast enuf, but I started him off agin, for I think he were in licker thro' a-sayin' as you was a-goin' out early.' 'So I am,' says father. I says, 'I'll go with you.' 'No,' he says, 'Martin will do; but where's my sticks?' I says, 'I've got 'em, and your clump-foot too, all right, so don't worret no more about 'em;' and downstairs I went, a-leavin' the door locked. And now I've come in to you, Mrs. Brown, jest to say as I've locked up all the 'ouse, and shan't come back for a 'our or two, and don't you mind if father makes a noise, cos he can't get out, and I'm a-goin' arter a servint."

I says, " All right; it ain't no business of mine, so shan't interfere."

" No," she says; " but as you're the only nay-bour, thro' the 'ouse the other side bein' to let, I thought I'd tell you not to mind 'is 'owls and 'am-merin's at the door."

I says, " All right," and out of the place she walks.

But law! she didn't know wot a desperate old waggerbone 'er father were, for I went to our back

7

door, and 'eard 'im at 'is winder, as were the one-pair back, a-shoutin' "Thieves!" and "Murder!" like anythink. So I didn't take no notice, but went in agin, and then I 'eard a knockin' at Sinful's front door, and looks out at my parlour winder, and see that impident young minx, as I knowed by sight, all dressed out, and a old fish-fag with 'er. So I went to the door, and says, "It's no use you're a-knockin', cos the lady 'ave gone out, and the old gent he's confined to 'is bedroom."

Says the gal, "Yes, I knows, and that's 'is wretch of a dorter's doin's."

I says, "Oh, indeed!"

"Yes," she says, "as is goin' to shet him up in a mad'ouse, and all for 'is bein' fond and faithful."

"Ah," I says, "I dessay, but I don't know nothink about 'is ways."

Says the old woman, "Would you mind lettin' a friend of ourn go thro' your premises and get over the wall, so as to get in the back way."

I says, "Oh, dear, no! I couldn't allow that, as might turn out burglars."

Says that young gal, "Ah, you're jest as bad as that old cat, 'is dorter, but," she says, "I'll 'ave 'im if I tears the door down to get at 'im, for he's my lorful 'usban'."

I busts out a-larfin', and says, "Your lorful grandmother! Why, he's jest on eighty!"

" He's only jest over sixty," she says, " as I considers in 'is prime."

" Yes," says the old woman, " in course it is, and this young gal doats on 'im."

" Ah," I says, " no doubt she's one of them as would rather be a old man's darlin' than a young man's slave; but," I says, " as to old Sinful, he did ought to be took up, a old beast. Why, she ain't sixteen !"

She says, " I'm nearly twenty."

" Ah," I says, " you're old enuf to know better, the same as 'im, but," I says, " you don't come thro' my place, that's all."

She says, " I'll have the door bust open."

I says, " You'd better. Ah," I says, " and 'ere comes Miss Sinful to 'elp you do it, as'll soon settle the pint."

And there, sure enuf, she was, and when she come up that gal were a-goin' to cheek 'er, but Miss Sinful she says, quite perlite, " Oh, pray walk in, Miss Sloper, I wanted to see you ; and will you come in too, Mrs. Brown ?"

So I says, " Certingly, if you wishes it ;" for I'm sure I never 'adn't 'ardly crossed the door friendly, and as to a cup of tea with 'em, why, I never 'ad so much as the smell of one in that 'ouse.

So we all walks into the parlour, and then Miss Sinful says, " Sarah Sloper, I thinks it right to tell you as my haged pa is a loonatic; there's the doctor's certificate, as I've been and fetched, so if you dares to come near this 'ouse agin I'll lock you up, and 'im too."

The gal begun a-whimperin' and a-cryin', but the old woman as were with 'er, she says, " Come on, it's no go," and takes and pulls 'er out of the room, and off they walks.

I says to Miss Sinful, " Your pa's uncommon quiet, and is up to mischief, no doubt, like the children always is, when not a makin' no row."

She say, " 'As he been uproarious."

I says, " I believe you, enuf to bring the injines, if it 'adn't been the back of the 'ouse."

So she goes upstairs, and opens 'is door, and give a yell as made me 'urry up, and if the room weren't empty and the winder open. I rushes to it cos she was took faint, and there I see old Sinful a-'angin' on to the hivy, as grows up the back of the 'ouse, jest over the waterbutt, with only 'is trousers on; I knowed it wouldn't be no use a-ketchin' 'im by the 'air, as were only a wig, as in course would come off in my 'and like a rat's tail, or the 'andle of a jug; so I makes a dive at 'im and gets 'old of 'is harm, as werry nigh pulled me out of the winder, but he couldn't 'it me for fear of leavin' go of the hivy. So I 'ollers to 'is dorter, " Don't set there a-faintin', but come and 'elp me

ketch 'old of some wulnerable part on 'im with the
tongs, and don't mind a-pinchin' 'im if it's to savo
'is life."

She jumps up, and jest then Mr. Cardwell,
as lives at the back, as is a rope-maker's walk,
he come over the palin's with a boy and a laddor,
'earin' me 'oller 'elp, jest in time to save that old
man from droppin into the waterbutt, as the lid
on were broken, for he were a-slippin' thro' my
fingers, and 'adn't no strength left to 'old on to the
hivy by no longer; we got 'im thro' the winder and
on to 'is bed, and the way as that old reprobate
cussed and swore at me, tho' in fear of 'is dorter,
were enuf to turn a Quaker's blood cold. So I
werry soon made myself scarce, as the sayin' is, and
'ome I went, and I don't believe as the old beast is
any more mad than me; and as to that doctor's
certificate, it were only to say as he were too old
to serve on the jury, and that I know as a fact.
She's a artful one is Miss Sinful, for she reg'lar
worked 'er own sister out of the 'ouse, as well as
that sister's child, not as I ever interferes in family
matters, but never arter that could I go out in my
gardin without old Sinful a-settin' at his back parlor
winder a-cussin' and swearin' at me, as were partly
the cause of me a-persuadin' Brown to move, as
said go and live on the top of the Monyment, so
long as you're 'appy and don't bother me; as made

me feel 'urt, and never in this world did I 'ave sich a-movin'; and then when clear out of the 'ouse to think of that old Sinful a-pursuin' any one with 'is spite all the way to close agin the Royal Hoak, as we moved to, cos it suited Brown to be near the Great Western; and a nice job it were for me, as 'ad one of them wans as moves you without no packin', tho' it give me a turn to see 'em tumble the things into it all undone, and didn't feel 'appy till I see it packed full and locked, and then went off in a cab with the cat in a band-box, and lots more light things besides. I'd sent Mrs. Challin on before with some odds and ends in a tilt cart as belonged to her niece's 'usband, as kep' a coal-shed close by, and wanted to move me altogether in spring wans. But Brown he's all for progress, he is, so would 'ave this ere new invention. So I got to the new place, as is a nice 'ouse enuf, close agin the 'Arrer Road, as leads to Kensil Green, so a cheerful spot, cos if there's one funeral a day as passes there's fifty, as always keeps the road lively. I took tea with Mrs. Padwick, as I were a-goin' to sleep at, and then went on to the new 'ouse, and waited and waited for that wan, but all in wain.

In course it ain't no use a-waitin for goods removed arter twelve o'clock at night, so then I give it up for a bad job, and went over to Mrs. Padwick's to sleep, tho' I'm sure it were a mockery to call it sleep, for I was nothink but dreams all night, and fancyin' fust as I 'ad got my drawers over my 'ead and on my chest, and then that I was bein' drove on a wan, a settin' on the top of my own beddin', as fell off behind with me; and then as Mrs. Challin 'ad got me down, and were a-tearin' out my back 'air with a carvin'-knife at my throat. So in course didn't wake up much refreshed in the mornin', and 'urried thro' my cup of tea, and gets over to our new place, but not a trace of no wan nor nothink, and my heart misgave me a-thinkin' the way as them fellers 'ad most likely treated my things, for the last time as I moved you'd 'ave thought as it were a earthquake as they'd under-went, at the werry least; and 'ow Mrs. Padwick could stand by and let 'em leave the bed-room in the settin'-room, with the 'andles knocked off right and left, and the settin'-room things took up to the garrets.

I see it weren't no use a-tryin' to do nothink but set on that washin'-tub and wait, and was a-wonderin' wot 'ad 'appened to poor old Challin, as 'ad started off over night reglar screwed; and I 'eard as the perlice collared 'er at the corner. Jest then came a knock at the door, as proved to be 'er, with a black eye like a addled hegg, as she said she'd 'it it agin the bed-post, a-gettin' up in a 'urry, so I see as she'd forgot all about overnight.

So I says, "Wherever did you sleep, then?"

She says, "Why, a friend give me arf a bed."

I says, "You're a lyin' old toad; I knows where you slep', as were the Perlice Station; so, you see, I knows all about it, as did ought to be ashamed of yourself, not to be trusted with the licker at your time of life."

She began a-wimperin', and sayin' it were nothink but fatigue.

"Well," I says, "let it be a warnin' to you, for next time they won't let you off so easy;" cos I could see with arf a eye as the perlice 'adn't meant to be 'ard on 'er, so let 'er out when she was sober.

"Well," I says, "turn to with your pail and flannin', and try and get a place ready for to set down the things when they comes in."

She did set to work with a will, as the sayin' is, and jest then there come a man to say as my things was took to the greenyard, thro' the 'orse and wan bein' left a-standin' at my door with no one to mind 'em.

Wot to do I didn't know, and then the feller if he didn't take and cheek me, as swore he'd got 'ere by eleven o'clock, and the place all locked up, and while he were gone to look arter me, as the perlice came and collared the lot; as was wot Mrs. Challin's nevvy 'ad brought the day afore, so pay 'im I wouldn't, for never did any one see sich a load of rubbish as he'd brought—old flower-pots, and blackin'-bottles, and things as that gal must 'ave put in for nothink but downright impidence; cos she was goin' to leave, as wasn't worth the carryin' downstairs, let alone bringin' away; and as to one chest of drawers, why, they was full of 'oles, with the back leg broke off, so wouldn't stand upright.

I could 'ave set down and 'ad a good cry over them things, only 'adn't no time to, for before twelve o'clock I 'ad the Queen's taxes, the gas, and the water all down on me, as was all owin'

So I says to the collector, "Then, wotever are you a-goin' to do?"

"Oh!" he says, "I shall distrain on the goods as is in, cos I knows you and 'ave been warned."

So I says, "Oh! indeed," a-seein' it were old Sinful's doin's, and give Mrs. Challin the wink for to get away with 'er pail, as I'd borrered of Mrs. Padwick, and I says, "Go to 'er and wait there for me."

So on 'em words of mine she lewanted on the quiet, and I goes back to that tax-gatherer and says, "I don't believe as it's law as I must pay, and shall go to my lawyer over it."

"Well," he 'says, "I shall leave a man in per-session."

I says, "All right," for I knowed as there wasn't ten shillings worth of things in the place, and out of the 'ouse I walks, and goes over to the man as 'ad moved me without packin' for to a⸱k why he'd been and detained my goods, tho' glad in my 'art he 'ad.

When I got to 'is place there was that big wan a-standin' under a shed all packed, and wot do you think, why, if that old impident waggerbone, Sinful, for I brought it 'ome to 'im, 'adn't out of spite not only rote to the tax-gatherer, but if he 'adn't been and told the owner of 'em wans as I didn't want the things for a day or two, and would let 'im know.

It was all right as it turned out, cos in course I was able to keep 'em back and reg'lar floor 'em rates and taxes; and so I did, for I left 'em to seize all the rubbish as were on the premises, and as I'd left the key with the man in persession I jest left the landlord for to do as he liked, as did ought to 'ave told me about them taxes bein' owin'

He come over to Mrs. Padwick's that werry evenin'- and squared it with me, so I rote a note, leastways Mrs. Padwick's niece did, for to tell that wan man to send the things.

You might 'ave knocked me down with a feather, as the sayin' is, when he come over and said as I shouldn't 'ave a stick till I paid 'im for 'is two wans, as would be forty-eight 'ours at three shillin's the 'our.

"Wot," I says, "seven pounds four! never in this world."

He says, "I'll take 'arf the money, and you don't get your goods till you pay it, and that's all about it."

I says, "I'll go to the majestret over it."

He says, "You may go to the devil for wot I cares."

I never was so dumfoundered, as the sayin' is, cos in course the willin' 'ad got the best of me thro' me 'avin' told 'im to keep 'em back; so I 'ad to pay the money, and we got the things unloaded, and they was a-many on 'em reg'lar pulverized; and it's a mussy as Brown weren't at 'ome or I shouldn't never 'ave 'eard the last on it.

And as to that fellow a-sayin' as he moved things without no packin', I'm sure that's true enuf, as 'adn't 'ad even a bit of mattin' put atween 'em to stop 'em from rubbin', and anythink like the weneer on my loo-table I never did; and the things all that dusty and scratched as I could 'ave 'ad a good cry over 'em; with a large stain on the middle of that parlour carpet as I don't believe as no ox-gall in this world won't never get it out.

So arter all I'd better 'ave paid 'em taxes at fust, as wasn't much over two pounds.

I was that knocked up when I'd got the things out of the wan, as was close on seven o'clock, and felt as do no more I couldn't that night, so I sends Mrs. Challin about 'er business, and locks the door, and goes over to Mrs. Padwick's to 'ave my supper, for I 'adn't 'ad no tea, and says to 'er, "Them things may take care of theirselves for to-night," as I'd got my bit of silver and a few things as I walued most along with me, and says, "I'll get to bed early," and so I did, 'opin' for a good night, a-makin' up my mind not to 'ave breakfast till 'arf past eight at the werry earliest next mornin', as I considers late even when you've nothink partikler to do like Sunday mornin', but the woice of the slug-gard, as the sayin' is, when you're busy. I'm sure I 'adn't been a-thinkin' about Disreely nor yet no other pollytics thro' bein' too busy all day, and whyever I should be a-standin' in a crowd as was all a-makin' a row and a-talkin' and a-sayin' as they'd come to wait on 'im, I can't think, as reached from Cherrin' Cross down to 'em two 'Ouses of Parlymint, so I says, "Bless my 'art," to a party as were a-standin' near to me, as I knowed to be Wolly tho' he'd got a false nose on, I says, "Wotever is up?"

"Oh," he says, "the British public as is reg'lar

outraged at me a-bein' sent to prisin for contempt of Court."

"Well," I says, "certingly you always was beneath contempt, in my opinion, and a poor old man as 'is 'armless tho' werry offensive; but," I says, "as to the British public a-carin' whether you're 'anged, drored, and quartered, as your betters 'as been afore you, don't you believe it, my boy."

"You be blowed," says a party, a-turnin' fierce on 'im, "who are you but a ass, as 'ave ruined heverythink as you touches."

"Come, come, Onsler," says Wolly, "don't you turn on me like that."

"Turn on you, I should like to stick you, to think of the money as I've lost thro' you, and my seat too."

Says a man, "I'm blessed if I don't 'ave my money, to set there for nearly two 'undred days on that bloated beast, and now not get paid arter all wot we was promised."

"But," I says, "Disreely can't 'elp that, cos it was Gladstin's lot as done it."

"Oh! it's all the same, there's six of one and 'arf a dozen of the other," says the Prince of Wales to me in a under tone, "here I am come with my wife and family for a depitation to ask old Dizzy to take the dooty off soap, cos washin' is downright ruin."

"Ah!" I says, "it do run into money, with a young family, and them small things mounts up like socks and sich like, tho' they take 'em by the dozen; and now suppose you don't like to 'ave the washin' done at 'ome, cos of that 'orty Rushin Duchess a-bein' able to see the things a-'angin' out from 'er winders in your back gardin, as don't make a 'ouse look well, I must say.

There was two fieldmales a-scrougin' me werry much, so I says, "Ladies, it ain't no good shovin'."

"Oh! ain't it," says one, "I knows better than that, don't I, Mrs. Tredgitt?"

"That you do, Mrs. Jury," said the other, "as is a ornyment to your sect, and rites sich lovely letters."

"You're another," said Mrs. Jury.

"Wotever are you a-doin' 'ere?" says I.

"Oh! we're a depitation," says Mrs. Jury, "to ask Disreely to let that there barrernite out of Millbank, as is the right man in the right place, and been a true friend to me; and as to my brother Charley, I should like to see 'im 'ung, a willin, as 'adn't no right to come and interfere with my little game, as was a-makin' a werry nice thing out of that there stout party, and he must come and want to be let into the little game, as I always were agin lettin' 'im in, and rote with my own 'ands to tell Wolly and Onsler not to give 'im nothink."

"Ah ! there ain't no justiss in this world," says Mrs. Tredgitt, with a sigh, "not even the Chief Justiss, as I've rote to with my own 'ands, and never 'ad tho perliteness to anser my letter, as can't be no gentleman, and means to rite to Queen Wictorier, if Disreely don't do a somethink for us."

"I say," says a woice, "you Martha Brown, you gib me back my umbreller."

I turns, and there were King Coffee and a lot of them denuded blacks of 'is all round. I says, "Go along with you, Queen Wictorier's got your umbreller, as is too much the lady to keep it now as you've come over here, cos it's a thing as you can't possibly do without in London. But," I says, " wotever made you come over 'ere with all this lot, and 'ardly no clothes on."

"Oh !" he says, "me come and see Massa Disreely, as am a depitation."

"If he don't give us Home Rule we'll be afther sayin' a word or two," says a Hirishman, close agin my ear, with a reg'lar crowd behind 'im.

I says, "Mussy on us, Doctor Cummin, surely you ain't of the Hirish persuasion ?"

"Ain't I tho', jewel," he says, with a wink, as made me turn away my 'ead for he've got a werry perswadin' eye, as I'm told he uses werry free in the pulpit.

"I will never rest till I get them iniquitous liquor

laws repealed," says a loud woice as was Archbishop
Mannin', "and I've jest walked down from Clerkenwell Green with ten thousand publicans at my 'eels,
and if Disreely won't receive us in a private room I
shall feel very much 'urt."

"Who are you?" says a fat man with a werry
low billycock 'at on, as I knowed were Spurgin, as
said, "I'm 'ere with all the costermongers in London
to wait on Disreely, cos we'll 'ave total abstinence,
cos we never touches nothink speritial ourselves
and nobody else shan't."

I says, "Don't you think to get your way, cos
Queen Wictorier in 'er own royal speech 'ave said
as she will 'ave 'em licker laws altered, not as in
course she ever wants to send for a quartern of
brandy in church-time thro' suddin' illness, but she
'ave a feelin' 'art, like a true queen; besides which
might be left without a drain in the 'ouse some day, or
in movin' about without 'er keys and want something
for a friend as dropped in promiscous. But," I
says, "mussy on us, you ain't all a-goin' to see that
poor man, Disreely, at once as will go distracted?"

For besides 'em others there was Cardinal
Wolsey and all 'is sojers come from the Gold Coast,
as said as the Merrykins 'ad been and swindled 'em
out of their loot. Then there was the 'igh priest of
the Jews and Petticoat Lane at 'is back, to petition
agin the Riteralists; and all the Bishops makin' a

row for to 'ave the 'Stablished Church put down, and the Wesleyans and Baptists they was all for church-rates; and the publicans, they would 'ave a heavy tax on all lickers. So I says, "Mussy on us, why, Bedlam broke loose, as the sayin' is, ain't nothink to this."

"It ain't indeed," says a woice, and there set poor old Dizzy, with 'is 'air in paper and 'is feet in 'ot water, and taller on 'is nose, reg'lar bunged up with a cold.

I says, "You 'ave got a nice one, you 'ave, old boy; but," I says, "don't keep in 'ot water too long."

"Oh!" he says, "I'm tryin' to get used to it, for it's wot I never expects to be out on any more."

"Ah! I see," I says, "and that's why you'vo tallered your nose, cos you fully espects as you'll 'ave to take kindly to taller to please tho Rooshins."

"Oh," he says, "there ain't much the matter with me, but if I was to get up and dress myself I should be killed with them depitations, as won't let me 'ave no peace, for I 'adn't 'ardly got into the hoffice, as Gladstin's lot 'ad left in a nice mess, I can tell you, when they come down on me like 'ale, as'll be a week's work to get the dustman to clear out the waste-paper and rubbish."

" Ah," I says, " if they comes round reglar, as is
wot they never does, and then won't take away
rubbish such as no doubt Gladstin 'ave left behind
not under sixpence sometimes, tho', if you takes my
adwice, you'll stick to tuppence every time as they
comes, and then don't give no Christmas-box."

Says Queen Wictorier to me, " Wot a manager
you are to be sure, Mrs. Brown ; I only wish I 'ad
your 'ead for business, for I'm sure you'd save me
a little fortin in kitchen-stuff alone."   But she
says, " Now, Benjamin, do look sharp and get on
with that there whitewashin' of yourn."

And I looks round, and there were Dizzy in a
white jacket and a paper-cap, a-standin' on a
box, on the top of a table, a whitewashin' the
ceilin'

" 'Ave you rote out that speech for me ?" says
Queen Wictorier.

" Why," says he, " you sent it back for me to
alter, and I've been and read it out to 'em."

" Well," says she, " and wot did they say ?"

" Why, some 'on 'em says as I've been and
copied it out of a old one as Gladstin rote for you."

" Yah ! and so you did," says Gladstin, a-lookin'
in at the winder, as were pushed down at the top.
" Yah ! I wouldn't be mean."

If Disreely didn't take and shake 'is whitewash-
brush all in Gladstin's face, as took and shied dirt

in at the winder, when up comes John Brown, and
give 'em a back'ander a-piece, as made Dizzy
blubber, and sent Gladstin a-'owlin' down the street
with 'is eye bunged up with whitewash.

So I says to Dizzy, "I must say as it serves
you both right, a-quarrelin' under Queen Wictorier's werry nose."

He says, " You ain't Queen Wictorier."

I says, " I never said I was ; but," I says, "she
were 'ere jest now, and is somewhere close at 'and,
for she's givin' a look round the premisis, and ain't
a-goin' to leave heverythink to you."

" Well, she ain't got much by leavin' things to
Gladstin," says he, "and I'm blessed if I stands
arf as that poor feller were obligated to put up with,
as I can't 'elp a-pityin' ; and as to 'Ome Rule, I
won't 'ave it, nor yet no Licker Laws."

" Well," says Queen Wictorier, a-puttin' 'er
'ead in at the door, " I tell you wot it is, somethink
must be done to stop this 'ere wife-murder ; a nice
thing it'll be for the Rooshins to read in the papers
the way as Inglishmen kills their wives, and jeers
over their dead bodies. Why, I shall 'ave the
Hemperor of Roosher a-sendin' a fleet up to 'Unger-
ford Wharf for to purtect 'is dorter, as will be
werry illconvenient for the penny steamers."

Says Spurgin, " Then why not 'ead a whisky
war, like Merryker ? cos it's all owin' to drink ; and

if you was to send Mrs. Brown at the 'ead of all the fieldmales in Ingland, she'd soon put it down."

I says, " Mrs. Brown wouldn't do nothink of the sort, cos she ain't a fool; no more ain't Queen Wictorier, as might as well make a law as them brutes should'nt 'ave no wives to murder, and so send all the women off to Horsetralia; cos as long as the world lasts parties will get drink some'ow; but," I says, "'ow about hedication and Christianity, as 'ave been all the go so many years? and I've 'eard parties myself a-talkin' about our bein' a favoured people."

" So we are," says Spurgin.

"Oh yes!" says all the Bishops, and Dr. Cummin, all a-settin' round a-groanin'

"Well," I says, " in my opinion you're no better than your naybours, tho' you ain't got to the Commune yet, as'll come if you don't look out sharp, and 'ave lots of perlice to purtect the rich agin the poor."

Says Dizzy to me, " Now, Mrs. Brown, as I've been and cleaned myself, wot would you 'ave me do?"

I says, " That's a puzzle, that is, as I can't make out, tho' my good gentleman he do often esplain to me all manner about polytics as I do not understand myself, tho' I can see as somethink is 'rong somewheres, the same as there was last Sunday

about Matilder Purblick's panier, thro' bein' all
over 'er left 'ip, as I couldn't set it right thro 'er
bein' as crooked as a ram's 'orn, as the sayin' is,
and only made it wuss in tryin' to do my best; for
in a-goin' to pull it into the middle of 'er waist
behind, if I didn't take and tear it out by the roots,
as she'd bought ready made, as made 'er bust into
tears, and call me a meddlin' old fool, as weren't
perlite, tho' I escused 'er, cos it were aggrawatin'
certingly, with 'er young man a-waitin' for 'er jest
round the corner, as dursn't 'ave 'im call at 'er own
'ome, thro' 'er father bein' that wiolent over the
Sabbith, as he makes the 'ouse a little 'ell upon
hearth all day long, thro' keepin' it that strict."

Says Dizzy to me, "I should like to see that
gal."

I says, "Well, you might, any Sunday evenin'
as you was to go to Spurgin's, for she never misses
'im."

"Why," he says, "he's gone to Rome."

"Ah!" I says, "I dessay."

"And they're goin' to give 'im a 'at," says
Dizzy.

"Not afore he wants one," says I, "for he'd a
blackguard thing on 'is 'ead last time as I see 'im;
but he looks a jolly sort, and 'im and the Pope will
be fust-rate friends, no doubt, cos he's that afferble
and will remind 'im of Archbishop Mannin'."

Says Dizzy, "I've got a great secret for you."

I says, "Wot is it?"

"Why," he says, "mum," and he give a wink; and jest then I woke up; and never did I feel more disappinted at it all bein' a dream, cos tho' I shet my eyes and tried for to finish that dream, it would not come back, tho' I couldn't 'ardly believe as all them parties as I'd seen was all dreams as I'd been and 'ad, arter talkin' to Queen Wictorier and Disreely, and them depitations, I was surprised, cos it's so singler for me to be a-dreamin' like that, and then wake up and go off agin, and still be a-dreamin' about the same things, tho' not where you left off. For it were jest five when I woke up, a-tellin' Dizzy all about poor Matilder's panier, cos I 'eard the church clock strikin', and wasn't long afore I were off agin, and there stood Disreely all dressed in 'is best, with a lovely button-'ole in 'is coat, but didn't go on with 'is secret, but as said, "Mrs. Brown, I'm a-waitin' for you."

I says, "Wot for?"

He says, "To make you my lorful wife."

I says, "Get along with you; you've been a-drinkin', as must 'ave been overnight, cos it's so early. Why," I says, "my good man, I'm a married woman, with a reglar trump for a 'usband."

"Ah!" he says, "but he don't 'arf apprecerate sich a downright treasury as he've got in you."

"Ah!" I says, "I knows as you're fust lord on it, but you don't get me to be your lady."

"Oh!" he says, "why not? We can get a diworce; and," he says, "I wants to ask you so many questions about all manner."

"Then," I says, "if you want a treasury, why not take and marry that there Baroness Coutts, as they do say is worth millyons upon millyons, and must be, I should say, by wot she gives away; not but wot she never didn't ought to 'ave built that there Columbier Markit, and if she'd 'ave spoke to me, I'd 'ave give 'er a straight tip over it, as the sayin' is. Not as ever I'll believe as she give the money to that there Ortin."

Says Dizzy, "Well, if you won't 'ave me I can't 'elp it, and must tell Queen Wictorier so, as 'ave set 'er 'art on it; and 'owever I'm to govern the country without you I can't think, cos Martha's got 'er 'ead on, as was 'er Majesty's own words to me in partin'."

I says, "I don't believe as ever Queen Wictorier would 'old with no diworces, cos I've 'eard say as she've left strict orders, as not one on 'em is ever to be let in to see 'er drorin'-room, and tho' one or two 'ave got in on the sly, she's 'ad 'em turned out, like Mrs. Johnson the other day; not as I knows anythink agin Mrs. Johnson."

Says Dizzy, "Why were she turned out?"

I says "'Owever, should I know, as only knowed

three parties in the name, as one were in the tripe
line, as might 'ave made a fortin, and gone to
court thro' 'er money, as is the way some gets
there; and I knowed Mrs. Johnson, as were a
corn-cutter, but she's dead, or might 'ave gone
there to look arter the royal foot, not as it's likely
as Queen Wictorier would 'ave 'er corns cut in the
drorin'-room; and then there were a Mrs. Johnson
in the second'and wardrobe line, but 'er langwidge
was such to me in buyin' a welvet mantle of 'er, as
didn't suit me, that if she used 'arf on it to Queen
Wictorier, she'd 'ave took and 'ad 'er turned out
like a knife, as the sayin' is, and right she is, in my
opinion." I says, "'er character were fly-blowed,
as the sayin' is, and a woman as 'ave disgraced 'erself, there's a end on 'er, she's jest for all the world
as if she lost a eye or a leg, and tho' parties may
pity 'er she must go blind one side, and on crutches
all the rest of 'er life, and be a outcast, and serve
'er right, she've been and made 'er bed, and she
must lay on it."

"Ah!" says a fieldmale, as Dizzy were a-talkin'
to over the bannisters, as he called Lady Twist,
a-lookin' at me quite savidge, "that's wot parties
says of me, and that's why I've been turned out."

I says, "And right they are, so now you take
and 'ook it back to Belgium."

"Yes," says a bishop, as was standin' by,

" you're right, Mrs. Brown, for she imposed upon me, as 'ave actually took 'er down to dinner and let my wife talk to 'er."

" Ah ! " says a party, " but it's lovely to 'ear them fallin' parties a-goin' about a preachin' and givin' of tracts."

" Take one, Mrs. Brown," says a fieldmale, as some spoke to in the name of Lawrer.

" No," I says, " thank you, I never were in your line, and don't want to begin; and as to preachin' I think the least said the soonest mended, as the sayin' is. Cos them as lives in glass 'ouses didn't ought to throw stones."

Says Queen Wictorier, a-callin' to me over the stairs, " Mrs. Brown, don't waste your time down there, over sich parties, as is only gammon with their tracts, and thinks as thro' givin' 'em they'll gets leave to come up and see me, but I ain't sich a green'orn ; so are you ready, cos we shall be late for the boat race."

" Well," I says, " we're a-goin' there, ain't we, in this 'ere werry bus as puts us down close agin Putney Bridge ? "

Says Queen Wictorier to me, " Buses is great conweniences."

" Ah ! " I says, " right you are, your Majesty, but," I says, " they might give us a little more room, and parties in general makes theirselves

werry unpleasant in 'em, cos when you gits in,
parties as is there aready, seems to consider you
quite a intruder, and won't make no room for you
neither side, and if you 'appens to be stout, there's
fools as sets a-grinnin', and some on 'em as considers theirselves clever illudes to your size, and
talks about plenty of room for a little one, and all
manner like that, and then objects to set straight,
and will turn round to look out of the winder, and
squeeze you up; and as to umbrellers, they're a
downright plague of Egyp', as the sayin' is.''

Says Queen Wictoricr, "I've got King Coffee's
all right.''

I says, '' Why, you give it to me.''

She says, '' Oh! that were only for the
moment, jest to throw dust into the Hemperor o
Roosher's eyes, and make 'im come down 'ansom,
as he certingly 'ave done.''

'' Ah!'' I says, '' so I see by the papers, and
am glad as 'is dorter is a-goin' to stick to 'er
religion, tho' she don't seem to care where 'er
children goes to; nor more don't their granpa, as
is wot I calls takin' liberties with conshence.''

Says Queen Wictorier to me, '' Well, you see,
Mrs. Brown, 'im and me never couldn't be werry
partickler about them things, with a lot of dorters to
marry, cos it makes sich a deal of bother in families.''

Says a stout party, as were a-settin' oppersite

a-eatin' of a bun, as Queen Wictorier said were Dr. Pusey, "Ah!" he says, "if only I 'ad my way, I'd soon settle it, for I'd make everybody agree with me, as ain't no Riteralist myself, tho' I likes it in others, and if only they make me Pope——"

"Escuse me," says Dr. Cummin, "I'm a-goin' to be the next one, as Beastmark 'ave promised me."

"I wish as you'd move your wet umbreller, as is all a-drippin' into my Oxford shoes," says Gladstin to a party as 'ad jest got in, as were Disreely.

"Move it yourself," he says, as was soaked thro' and out of temper.

"You're no gentleman," says Pusey to the party next 'im, "to take and use my 'ankercher."

"I never said I was," says Cummin, "and only wiped my mouth with the corner on it."

"And right you are," says I, "cos self-praise ain't no recommendation, but," I says, "don't talk so loud, or you'll wake Queen Wictorier, as is noddin' in the corner of the bus."

"Fares for Wictorier," says the conductor, and both Gladstin and Dizzy 'ollers out, "We'll pay for 'er."

"I can pay for myself," says Queen Wictorier, awakin' up.

I says, "Don't pay 'im nothink, as 'ave brought us wrong, as ain't goin' to Putney at all."

"You got in at the Marble Harch," says the
feller, out of the crowd, awaitin' to see the Royal
marridge go by.

"Ah!" I says to Queen Wictorier, "they'll
be nicely sold, won't they?"

Says Gladstin, "I'm reg'lar sold."

"But," I says, "where's Queen Wictorier got to,
as were up in that corner a minit ago."

Says a sojer a-settin' next me, "Which is my
nearest way to Winsor?"

"Law," I says, "why, you must be Cardinal
Wolsey, as 'ave come over from A shanty in Africer.
But wotever did you bring them nasty, naked,
black beasts with you for, as nearly frightened poor
Mrs. Bewley to death, as 'll come round 'er while
a-lookin' in a shop winder in the Strand last Saturday night."

He says, "In course they're all black, as is
decent mornin' for their friends as 'ave been killed
in battle."

I says, "I won't stop in the bus with fellers as
ain't got no proper clothes ou. Let me out," I says,
"let me out," and I were a-fightin' like mad for to
get past all them blacks, as was a-settin' on other
parties' knees, and 'adn't nothink 'ardly on 'em but
shells and feathers, as is very well for fishes or
birds, but ain't proper for Christshuns to go about
n, tho' they are black by natur'.

Well, jest then a woice says, "It's time you was a-gettin' up, mum, I think," and who should it be but Mrs. Challin', as 'ad come with a tap, for I told 'er to call for me 'twixt eight and nine, and Mrs. Padwick 'ad made 'er 'ave a cup of tea along with 'er gal; so up I jumps, and when I'd got down, on we went to my new place, as is jest four streets off; and when we got into the street, the fust thing as met my eye were the outside of the 'ouse, a skelinton, reg'lar gutted, with two firemen at the door.

I did not drop cos I felt it were a dooty to 'old up, and if they didn't say as that place 'adn't took fire jest arter ten o'clock, and was down by eleven o'clock, thro' the ingins not a-comin' till it were nearly out, as burnt fast thro' its bein' a old dried-up house.

But whoever set it alight, I can't think; and it's a mussy as we wasn't all burnt in it, as we should 'ave been but for the things not a-comin' in, as shows 'ow little we knows wot's best for us in this world; so I did feel that thankful, partickler as Brown 'ad been and transferred the insurance afore he left town, so we got all the money, and tho' there was things as I walued more than money's worth, yet arter all, to 'ave everythink new and clean ain't so bad, so you see as one move were as good as a fire to me, as the sayin' is, but am

sure as that fire were foretold in my dream, cos
Queen Wictorier in a bus must 'ave meant somethink out of the way, cos tho' too much the lady
to look down on a bus, yet no call to get into one;
not but wot she'd enjoy it, for I will say as I've
'eard conwersations in them public conweniences as
is quite equal to Parlyment, and a deal better manners; and that's where I fust 'eard about Mrs. Tredgitt and Mrs. Jury, as is ladies anyone must allow,
and a pleasure to know, as shows if Ortin's ain't
a family of barrernites, they did ought to be, and
'ave their rights; and as to that their feller in Mil-
bank bein' ashamed of 'is name, and not a-answerin'
to it, why, I'd keep 'im on bread and water till he
did; as did ought to be proud on it, and partickler
'avin' sich a brother and sisters, as would go thro'
fire and water for 'im, and will do so yet, no doubt.

But we ain't a-goin' to furnish agin jest yet, me
and Brown, so am a-stayin' along with Mrs. Padwick, for he's backards and forards constant now;
and she's got a werry nice bed-room with a four-
poster, as is wot I wouldn't trust myself in everywhere, but ain't afeard through knowin' 'er 'abits,
as is took down every spring and every crevice
looked into, besides a room as I can set in, with a
bird's-eye view of the underground railway, as is
too far off to shake the house, tho' I can feel a
tremblin' when in bed sometimes as reminds one of

a earthquake a-rumblin', as is 'ow I come to dream
as Disreely were Guy Fox, and a-goin' to blow up
Parlyment cos they wouldn't listen to Gladstin, as
he let me into the secret over a cup of tea, as we was
takin' quite friendly, that real as I could 'ave swore
as I might 'ave pinched 'im, so in course told Queen
Wictorier, as stopped 'im, as I must 'ave dremt,
cos I'd been down to Parlyment for to see them members all a-comin' to 'ear wot Queen Wictorier 'ad
got to say for 'erself, tho' in course she didn't come
'erself, and she only says wot they puts in 'er mouth,
dear creature, as wouldn't 'arm a fly. So me and
Mrs. Padwick 'ad went down arter a early cup of
tea and stood about for to see them members a-
goin' in, tho' we only saw a few, as was werry dis-
appintin', and 'ad gone 'ome by the bus a-readin' of
the Queen's speech in a hevenin' paper, as was jest
the same as 'earin' it from 'er own lips, and I must
say as I were pleased at 'er illudin' to them licker
laws, as shows she've got a feelin' 'art, as can look
with a eye of pity on any one as is famishin' for 'arf
a pint, and tho' the Archbishop of Canterberry is a-
goin' to give up intoxicatin' drinks cos of 'is 'ealth
sufferin' thro' em, that ain't no reason as others
shouldn't 'ave a friendly glass like Archbishop
Mannin' as is the cup that cheers but don't inebriate,
as the sayin' is, and can smile and look that
cheerful over a cup of tea jest the same as a bowl of

punch; as shows a light 'art, and not one as the
look on is enuf to freeze a pump, or turn all the milk
in a dairy, as is jest the way with some, and always
were Mrs. Ockley's looks, as 'ad a milk-walk, as
were ugly enough, goodness knows, without the
forrin aid of horniment, as I'm sure that brown front
of 'ern didn't take a year off, but rather put a many
on, not as ever she 'ad any cause to be jealous of
me, goodness knows, tho' Ockley 'ad a charfin'
way with 'im over the new-laid eggs as I
did use to 'ave once on a time a good many on thro'
a-sendin' 'em to Lady Wittles's dorter as were always
a-layin' on a deal board thro' 'er spine a-growin'
out, but I'm sure while she were above ground I
don't think as Ockley 'ad made up 'is mind for a
minit about 'is second, tho' bein' a decent man in 'is
ways, as no one couldn't call a man or a woman
either, as had agreed to marry agin afore the breath
was out of 'er body, as was, Jane Selfort's disgustin'
ways, as were engaged three months afore she berried 'im, but always thinks it was 'er old fish-fag of
'er mother as put 'er up to it; tho' not one to interfere with my neighbours' affairs myself, tho' a dooty
sometimes to give any one a 'int in the right direc-
tion as might save the innercent, and make the
guilty tremble, as the sayin' is; like I did Miss
Sinful, and that's 'ow it were as I knowed about
that there Jem Slaney's tricks, as nothink couldn't

escuse, cos in course tho' Mrs. Alders were a fool, as I always considered 'er, and a deal too much chapel-goin' for me, with a bundle of wood short; and as to light weights, she were known by it all over the place, and fined three times, as is 'ow she was able to dress that smart, as don't look well at 'er time of life, not as that's any business of mine, but will never stand by and see willany, not done by my greatest enemy, tho' I don't consider 'er as such, but never dealt with 'er no more arter that duffin five-shillin' piece as she passed on me, and then denied to on 'er oath.

I always 'ad my suspicions as she were a-goin' to marry agin, thro' a-suspectin' at one time as there were a somethin' on the trapeze, as the French says, atween 'er and Mr. Ockley, the cow-keeper, as soon as he were a widerer, tho' no mourner, and not even pretendin' to as 'ow ever he should be, I can't think, for of all the women to go on, it were 'is late wife, and better late than never, as the sayin' is, for she was years older than 'im, and might 'ave lived to see 'im under the sod; but the cramps was too many for 'er, a-settlin' in the 'art, so didn't lay many weeks from the time as she took cold at the back-door a-watchin' 'im a-givin' out the milk, as was all 'er jealous ways without no foundation, but a strong easterly wind a-blowin' with a drivin' rain, as settled 'er 'ash under a month, as the sayin' is.

But never did I think as Mrs. Alder would take
and marry 'er own prentiss, a mere boy in the name
of Slaney, not out of 'is time, and a poor bit of a
whipper-snapper with weak eyes, as did used to
come round with a pair of sleeves on, and the soap
and candles, thro' 'er bein' in the chandlery line, as
was a fine business, tho' a poky shop in Alder's
time, but soon come to ducks and drakes, as the
sayin' is, with a boy of eighteen for the master on
it, as weren't fit for a prentiss.

Nicely she paid for 'er foolishness, as would 'ave
'im tho' 'is own father forbid the banns twice, and
dragged 'im forcible out of the church into a four-
wheel cab, but managed to give 'im the slip, and was
married at the Register arter all.

She 'adn't been 'is wife not three weeks afore
he begun for to show 'is clover foot, as the sayin'
is, as was drink and late 'ours, and never a-keepin'
to 'is chapel, as he were that reg'lar at, three times
a day Sunday and twice a week afore marriage, as
was what made 'er fancy 'im—leastways, so she
said; and then to find 'im a mask of deception as
'ad been a-keepin' company with two young gals,
and deceived both, as was their own faults, and
little did they think as me a-livin' over in South
Lambeth should know all about Mrs. Alder, as lived
close agin the London 'Orspital, and come to blow
the gaff, as the sayin' is.

But 'ow I come to find it out, were thro'
a-walkin' in the Boro' one evenin', and askin'
the price of some bits of floor-cloth at a broker's,
as said he'd some smaller bits inside, thro'
what was at the door bein' too large for what I
wanted.

So I steps inside, with my back to the door,
a-waitin' for 'im to reach 'em down when I 'ears
a woice as I thought I knowed, ask the price of a
chest of drawers.

The man asked me to escuse 'im a instant, and
goes to answer the party as was in a 'urry.

I was a-standin' by a shower-bath as 'ad cur-
tings round it, and a-lookin' thro' 'em who should
I see but that Jem Slaney along with Ann Sanders.
I stood and watched 'em, and that broker kep' on
a-talkin' and a-chaffin' on 'em over gettin' married,
as I 'eard 'er say, with my own ears, as their
banns was a-goin' to be put up the next Sunday
arter.

Well, I was a-thinkin' what I should do, but let
'em walk on, merely a-remarkin' to that broker
when they was gone as, "A many got married as
was sorry for it arterwards."

He said as, "That were true, but," he says,
"they're the right sort, for I knows the chapel as
he attends werry reg'lar, and 'er too, for that
matter."

"Ah!" I says, "indeed!" and 'avin' got the two little bits of oil-cloth as I wanted for two washin'-stands, I walks myself off.

I must say as I were sorry for the gal, as I knowed were in a shop in Newington Butts, and come 'ome every other Saturday to 'er mother in our street; and as to that waggerbone, I should like to 'ave rung 'is neck tho' I didn't pity 'is fool of a wife, not a bit, as were old enough to be 'is grandmother, so a-thinkin' as she didn't need no warnin' I made up my mind as I'd only go and tell Mrs. Sanders, as I'd know'd from gal'ood, as one might say, tho' not one as ever I'd made a friend on, thro' bein' full of 'er lies and braggindoshier, as the sayin' is; for when she were a-goin' to marry Sanders, as was only a workin' brazier, she give out as he were quite the gentleman and would ride in his carriage some day, and so he did sure enough, and the Queen's too, tho' only the perlice-wan, for he was in with a lot of bank-note forgers, and got penal servitude for five years over it.

I 'adn't set eyes on 'er for years, when I see 'er a-standin' at the door of a 'ouse close to mine, and spoke friendly, as told me she was a-livin' there, 'avin' took 'arf the 'ouse; not as I wanted for to be intimate like with 'er agin, a well knowin' what a tongue she'd got for abusin' anyone, as I'd felt it myself, so give 'er a wide berth, as the sayin is ever arter, not a-likin' any one as will fly out at you like ravin' bulls for nothink; leastways only a slip of the tongue as mine were quite unintentional.

For me and 'er, tho' neighbours near Stepney Church, 'adn't spoke for over two years thro' 'er a-takin' offence over me a-makin' a joke about a five-pound note as I were a-gettin' change for when 'er and me was out a-shoppin' together one day, and says to the young man as took it, and asked me to put my name on the back, " Oh, it's all right!" I says, " for we ain't no smashers, are we, Mrs. Sanders?" never givin' a thought about 'er 'usban'

She didn't say nothink till we got into the street and then give it me 'ot, and bounced 'erself into a bus as were a-passin', a-leavin' me 'arf putrified on the pavement, and never know'd as she'd been and moved to over the water thro' a-losin' sight of 'er, till that day.

So tho' perlite, we didn't say nothink much to one another for she's a 'aughty spirit, so I 'ave myself for that matter, and wouldn't stoop for to poke my nose into any one's door not wanted, and that's why as she'd never let me know as she lived there, as 'ow she could do it I can't think, as 'arf the 'ouse would run into money, as I'm sure she couldn't never afford with 'im 'avin' deserted 'er afore he took to forgin', not as ever she was one to

complain, and 'eld 'er 'ead that 'igh a-goin' out
a-marketin' with only a redicule, and never looked
in passin' our door, tho' next door but three.

So I was a-askin' Brown what he thought about
me a-tellin' Mrs. Sanders, as only says, " Please
yourself, as 'ill get no thanks for your pains."

I says, " And don't espect none thro' doin' a
dooty, as I considers it to try and save a young
gal."

" Well," he says, " that's right, that is, only be
sure as you can't save 'er if she wont save 'erself ;
but any'ow, you'd better let the mother know."

And so I did, a-'ritin' 'er a note that perlite, as
were word for word only this—

" Mrs. Brown begs for to inform Mrs. Sanders as
it's my opinion as your daughter Ann is a-keepin'
company with a married man in the name of Slaney.
So no more at present, from yours obedient."

I sent the note in by the gal on the Saturday
thro' bein' so near, and it wasn't not more than
'arf-past nine Monday as Mrs. Sanders come in,
a-flamin' like a turkey-cock, as the sayin' is, and
says, " Did you send me this scrawl ?" a-'oldin' out
my note.

I were a-standin' at the door when she come up
a-speakin' to the butterman, as 'ad brought me
downright cart-grease, so I says to 'er, " Step
inside, mum, if you've got anythink to say, as I do

not 'old with brawls as disturbs the street, and should be peace at 'ome."

She says, "I don't want to come into your place."

"Well then," I says, "stop out," and I takes and shets the door in 'er face, as in course I knows ain't actin' like a lady, in the reg'lar way, but I couldn't 'ave 'er standin' there a-'ollerin' at me.

She called me all the old fish-fags as she could lay 'er tongue to thro' the key 'ole, and made that butterman's boy shout with larfture all down the street.

It couldn't 'ave been more than eleven, when bein' werry busy with starchin' a few fine things in the front kitchen, the gal come and said as there were a lady as wanted me immediate.

So I didn't wait for to do more than dry my 'ands, and up I goes, and there set Mrs. Alder, leastways Mrs. Slaney I should say, with a wail down, a-sobbin' like mad.

I says, "Whatever is the matter?"

She says, "You knows all about it, Mrs. Brown, so don't deceive me."

I says, "About what?" a-guessin' as she were illudin' to that scamp of 'ern.

"Oh," she says, "my James, my beloved 'usban', my own dear."

I says, "What's to do with him?"

"Why," she says, "he's dead and gone, and drownded hisself, or wuss."

"Law," I says, "you don't say so."

"Yes," she says, "and all thro' you."

I says, "Thro' me, why I ain't set eyes on 'im since last Friday, when I see 'im in the Boro', along with Ann Sanders a-buyin' furnitur"

She give a shriek and says, "It's false, he were true as steel, and doated on the ground as I walked on."

I couldn't 'ardly 'elp a-bustin' out a-larfin in 'er face, but in course kep' my feelin's under, as she went on for to tell me as he 'adn't been 'ome for three days nor nights, and 'ad sent 'er a note a-sayin' as 'is days was numbered, and as Mrs. Brown 'ad been and pisoned 'is esistence with 'er base false'oods.

I says, "Me pison 'is esistence, as 'ave never give 'im bit nor sup, as the sayin' is, not since a bit of bread and treacle over nine year ago. 'Owever could I do it, my good soul."

"Well, she says, "he means as you're made 'is mind miserable."

"Made 'is mind miserable, indeed ; I suppose he means, thro' a-tellin' that poor gal's mother, as he were a married man, tho' nothink but a shop-boy."

Well, that put the old fool out, for she says,

"I thank you to speak respectful of my 'usban';
for I won't set and 'ear 'im run down not dead nor
alive."

I says, "I don't want to run 'im down, tho' I'm
pretty sure he's not dead."

While we was a-talkin', in bounces Mrs. Sanders,
without, with your leaf, or by your leaf, as the sayin'
is, and says "Mrs. Brown, where's my gal?"

I says, "Bother your gal and you too. 'Ow
should I know, as 'aven't see nor 'eard nothink of
'er, as I were a-tellin' Mrs. Slaney 'ere since Friday
last."

"Then," she says, "what does she mean by
ritin' on a bit of paper, 'Mother, I'm gone, and
Mrs. Brown will tell you all about it.'"

I says, "Mrs. Brown only knows what she's
told you, and 'ere sets that feller's good lady to
speak for 'erself; but," I says, "when did you miss
her?"

She says, "Not 'arf a 'our ago, as left this bit
of paper with old Mrs. Chaldrin, as lives jest round
the corner, and comes in for 'arf a day's charin',
a-tellin' 'er not to give it me till to-morrer, as did
'er dooty in a-comin' with it right straight off."

"Well then," I says, "she can't be got far,
and," I says to Mrs. Slaney, "when did you see
your beauty last?" as kep' on a-weepin' and a-wailin'
as I couldn't 'ardly understand 'er, as only 'eld out

the note as she'd got from 'im accusin' me of pison-
ing of 'is esistence.

I looks at the antelope and sees as it was the
London post-mark, and posted the werry night
afore; so I says, "Well, he ain't gone far for to
do it."

Then I asks Mrs. Chaldrin, as follered Mrs.
Sanders in, when Ann Sanders 'ad given 'er the
note, as was a-standin' on the mat all of a trimble,
as said as it were not a 'our ago.

"Well then," I says, "it's my opinion as they've
agreed for to meet somewheres this mornin', and I
do believe as the Boro' is their 'aunts, and," I says,
"that's where you'll ketch 'em, and," I says, "I'll
go with you and show you the spot, as I see 'em
a-walkin' together, and 'card 'em ask the price of
some things at a broker's shop."

Says Mrs. Sanders, as 'er pride 'ad come down,
"No doubt as you're right, for yesterday was 'er
Sunday 'ome, and I told 'er about your note the
first thing yesterday mornin', as I got it Saterday
evenin', and wouldn't say nothink on the Sabbath.

I says, "Did she go to chapel last night?"

"Oh!" she says, "yes, and wouldn't miss it
were it ever so."

"Ah!" I says, "then that's it; now," I says,
"let's go to the Boro ;" and off we started, and goes
to that broker's shop, leastways, I did, with Mrs.

Slaney and Mrs. Sanders a-waitin' round the corner.

I asks the price of a clothes-'orse as were at the door, as were a thing I were a-lookin' out for, as that broker said would not suit me, thro' a-wantin' new 'inges, as he would put for a trifle.

So I says to 'im quite casual-like, "'Ave them young parties got married yet, as was 'ere last week about the drawers."

"Well," he says, "it's my opinion as they was to be this werry mornin', for he was in the westry of our chapel last night, and said as he were a-goin' abroad for a time, and was a-goin' to take tracts for to conwert the natives."

"Law," I says, "wherever can he be a-goin', among wild savages like that?"

"Oh, no," he says, "it's the Catholics as he's a-goin' to conwert, as is full of their superstishuns over there."

I says, "Where about, I wonders?"

Jest then he says, "Why, there they both are in a cab, a-goin' to chapel, no doubt." And sure enuf there they both was.

I says, "Take a cab, and go along with this lady," for Mrs. Slaney 'ad came up to the door, "and foller 'em up, for," I says, "it's life and death; and will be somethink 'andsome in your pocket."

He were off like a shot, and me and Mrs.
Sanders got another cab and follered, and got to the
chapel just in time to see sich a scrimmage, for there
was Slaney as pale as death, with 'is face all scratched
and 'is 'air upset, and there was the minister a-'oldin'
Mrs. Slaney's arms, as 'ad been a-pitchin' into
'im ; and as to poor Mary Ann, she were flat on the
floor a-kickin', with the broker a-tryin' to distrain
'er with 'is knee, so me and Mrs. Sanders took and
picked 'er up, and 'er mother give 'er a good shake
and pulled 'er out of the place and into the cab, as
took 'er 'ome. I wouldn't go along with 'em, cos
I says, " Now I've done my dooty, I'm off, so no
more from me, as may settle it your own way," as
no doubt they will, thro' bein' all chapel-goers
together, as 'ave got their own notions about rite
and wrong, and is licensed for to marry jest as they
pleases, and can get divorced when they likes ; and
some, now-a-days, gets diworced, and then makes
it up, and marries one another over agin, as is
plenty of work for the lawyers and parsons any'ow,
so that's why I never interferes with no naybors,
tho' I've got a name for it.

But as to politics, I feels quite out of my elefant,
as the sayin' is, tho' I'm sure I read enuf about 'em
as is why they runs in my 'ead that constant of
nights. And see Disreely reglar 'auntin' me;
a-sayin' three nights a-runnin': " Mrs. Brown,

these 'ere depitations will be the death on me, do see some on 'em for me," and there he were standin' with 'is back agin the room door, as parties was a-tryin' to shove open. He says, "I won't let 'em in. Oh! pray come, Mrs. Brown, and throw your weight agin it; for it's the Fenians a-tryin' to get out of prisin."

"Wot," I says, "them wretches as blowed up the wall in Clerkenwell, and killed and injured innercent people in their own 'omes, let alone the furnitur as were blowed to bits." So I puts my back agin the door, a-runnin' at it backard with all my force, and then some one give a yell, as said "Oh! my fingers."

I says, "Who's got 'is fingers there?" And if it weren't Gladstin, as said he were a-goin' to adwise three courses; but, law! he were cut short by Queen Wictorier, who said, "Am I Queen, or am I not, Mrs. Brown?"

I says, "In course you are, your Majesty."

Then she says, "I won't 'ave the publics all shet up in this way, for 'owever is parties as 'ave been a-standin' in the snow for 'ours a-seein' me and my new dorter-in-law, as I'm proud on, go by, to stop out arterwards and see the 'luminations, if they can't get a drop of supper beer when they gets 'ome, tired as dogs, as the sayin' is?"

I says, "Bless your royal 'art, as is a true-born

Britten to your backbone, and won't stand by and
see us done out of our beer, as 'ave brought up
millyons as is ready to shed their last drop for you;
and a nice thing if them troops as landed at Ports-
mouth couldn't 'ave got a cool pint a-piece at
the werry least, the moment as they got ashore, for
to drink your Majesty's 'ealth; and no doubt old
Cardinal Wolsey 'isself and 'is good lady opened
their shoulders over a pot with a 'ead on, as they
must 'ave injoyed arter that 'ot Afriker, as is all
sand and fevers, I've eard; but," I says, "I really
can't stop a-gossipin' 'ere, for I've promised to go
into Parlyment along with Mrs. Padwick."

Says Dizzy, "Look sharp, old gal, and they'll
elect you Speaker."

I says, "Young man, don't you make that free
a-callin' me old gal, cos," I says, "tho' your 'air do
curl that lovely, you needn't look down on them as
'ave been drove to fronts thro' fevers, or as I knowed
poor Mrs. Whistin, as went to 'ave 'er 'air done;
and if the willin' didn't take and cut large lumps
off behind, and then say as it were a-fallin' off thro'
weakness, and persuaded 'er to 'ave 'er 'ead shaved
for to strengthen it, as never growed agin above
arf a inch, and there she were landed, as the sayin'
is, with a bald 'ead to 'er dyin' day, as 'ad that
lovely back 'air as she could set on it, leastways so
she did used to say, tho' I never see a westment on

it. But, law bless me!" I says to Dizzy, "I never 'ad sich a turn as in goin' down Parlyment Street, for who should I see but a milingtary party as were sweepin' a crossin' in full uniforms and all 'is medals; so I says, 'Who is he?' 'Oh!' says a Bobby, 'that's the Dook of Cambridge, as can't get no justiss out of the 'Orse Guards, so 'ave been and punched the Bishop of London's 'ead as he walked by, and then took to 'is broom, and is a-waitin' for Queen Wictorier to pass, as will, no doubt, throw 'im some coppers, poor fellow, as must feel 'urt, arter all as he've done for 'is country, not to get 'arf pay even, and see others put over 'is ead.'" So I turns round, and if there wasn't Disreely on 'is legs, a-speakin' beautiful, with Gladstin a-settin' oppersite 'im, a-jeerin', and sayin' "'Ear, 'Ear!"

So Disreely says to me, "Jest you take notice, Mrs. Brown, cos Queen Wictorier will believe you."

"Yes," I says, "but 'ow about the Prince of Wales' 'avin' more money? Now, as that there Hemperor of Roosher 'ave come down so 'andsome with 'is dorter, let's up and show as we ain't beggars; and if we've got a royal family, and a fine one, we means to keep 'em as such."

Says the Hemperor of Roosher, a-leanin' over my chair, "Martha, my dear, I can give wot I likes,

for I ain't got no tinkers and tailors as calls theirselves Parlyment to bully me; and if I 'ad Gladstin and Disreely a-darin' to come and talk to me
'arf a word of wot they says to Queen Wictorier,
I'd order 'em a round dozen a-piece, and send 'em
to Siberier, as is where the pickled crabs come from,
jest to cool their backs."

I see Dizzy turn pale and Gladstin give a shiver
at 'is words. So I says, "You two boys needn't
be afeard; he don't touch a 'air of your 'eads."

Says Dizzy, "I think you might as well 'ave said
a curl, and not 'ave mixed up my 'air with them
grizzly rat's tails of old winegar wisage oppersite."

I says, "Don't be personal, as didn't make hisself, and ain't got time to put 'is 'air in paper every
night the same as parties as shall be nameless." I
'eard a noise and looks round, and there were
Queen Wictorier in all 'er robes a-settin' jest like
waxwork for loveliness, as says, "My Lords and
Gentlemen,—I'm 'appy to meet you agin in Parlyment, as is only a mere matter of form, and some
says a farce, as is a espression as didn't ought to
'ave been put in my royal mouth, cos I don't go to
plays now-a-days, any more than Mrs. Brown, as
tells me she once 'ad a buster over it." I were that
pleased at bein' illuded to in the Queen's Speech, as
made me say 'ear and 'ear, and 'it the ground with
my umbreller.

Disreely give sich a shriek, and says, " Oh ! 'ang it," tho' that weren't esactually the word, "my bunion," as made Gladstin bust out a-larfin'

I says, " Do be quiet, for I can't 'ear the Queen's Speech."

" Why, you've got it in the papers," says Dizzy.

" Law," I says, " 'ow can they 'ave it there when it ain't all spoke yet."

" Why," says Gladstin, " he sent it afore'and to the papers as is on 'is side."

" Well, then," I says, " if I was Queen Wictorier I'd say quite different to wot was put down, and sell the lot on you."

Says Queen Wictorier to me in a whisper, " So I do, Martha ; for bless you, not one on 'em can rite Inglish, leastways, not Queen's Inglish."

" Ah ! " I says, " and mark my words if they ain't all in the swim with that old Beastmark, as wants to turn us all into Germans, as is a 'ard lot, and won't let the children be taught no prayers, leastways so I were a-readin' in the papers last year, as they'd been and stopped one of their ministers as said as prayers was good things for children. I've 'eard as a many over there is like that, and must make you feel werry un'appy about your grand-children, not that both your dorters 'as been that well brought up as no Germans can't do them any 'arm." So Queen Wictorier didn't make no anser,

but walked off quite strong and 'arty with King
Coffee's umbreller under 'er arm, as she said she
were a-goin' to leave at South Kensinton for old
King Cole to 'ave a look at it; for she says he is a
jolly old soul.

"Ah!" I says, "and looks it too, and 'ave done
a deal of good too, any'ow for 'is friends, as is wot
I likes in a man, for as to sayin' as there ain't to be
no jobbery, nor bribery in the world, why, that's
all foolishness, as always was and always will be;
but if you 'ave got anythink to give away, why, give
it your friends if they wants it, and can do the
work as well as anybody else."

"Ah!" says Queen Wictorier, "I do wish as
you could persuade somebody for to let me 'ave
more to give away, for I've got such a trifle as it's
almost a insult to offer it."

"Yes," I says, "so I've 'eard say, and them as
gets it werry often ain't them as wants it; but," I
says, "no doubt Dizzy will see to all that, if they
don't pester 'im to death with them depitations, as
is I considers downright cruelty to animals."

He says, with a sigh, "I tell you wot it is, Mrs.
Brown, my life ain't worth 'avin' at the price, and I
don't want to worret poor Queen Wictorier more than
I can 'elp, but really if I'm to be bothered all day
long with the butchers and bakers and candlestick
makers, I might as well be Lord Mare at once."

" You don't dine with me," says the Lord Mare,
a-poppin' up 'is 'ead.

" You needn't be so savidge with 'im," says
Gladstin, " he ain't a Oxford man."

" Oh! ain't he," says the Lord Mare, " that
makes a difference, for I considers them Oxford
men a low-lived crew." I turns round and see one
or two of them young fellers in their dark blues
a-standin' by, and I says, " My dear boys, whyever
not 'ave sent a perlite note to say as you couldn't
send a reglar anser, cos in course, them others
a-answerin' that ready, put you to a non plush, as
the sayin' is; cos in course they was all agreed
about goin' and you wasn't, but you did ought to
remember as he meant well, did that Lord Mare,
and tho' in course arter that wiolent hexercise as
you've been a-takin', you likes to be quiet all the
hevenin', and don't want no dinner but a mutton
chop or hegg with your teas together, jest to show
as there ain't no mallis atween you when the fight
is over, like true Hinglishmen."

Says a woice close to me, " I wonder which will
win the day; three to one on Dizzy; pull away old
flick." " Go it, sweet Willyim," says another; and
there I see Dizzy in one boat, and Gladstin in
another boat, with nothink on but their jerseys and
bare arms, a-pullin' like wild, and parties a-'oorayin'
on land, then all of a suddin Gladstin's oar took

and snapt right in 'arf, and over he went backards.

I says, "He's a dead man, 'elp," I says, "'elp, he's a-drownin'."

"Why, mussy on us, wot's the matter," says Queen Wictorier, a-givin' me a violent shake, and a-sayin' "wake up, Martha," and so I did, and there was Mrs. Padwick, as 'ad brought me a cup of tea, thro' me 'avin' gone to bed with a bad 'ead-ache, as were all thro' me a-standin' about so long the day afore, a-seein' of Parlyment assemblin', as weren't much of a sight, cos Queen Wictorier didn't go, as I 'eard a party say in the crowd she couldn't abear them Tories about 'er.

I says to 'im, "My good man, Queen Wictorier is too much the lady, not to bear them, as it's their dooty to come about 'er, and," I says, "as to Tories, why, they've been and berried along with their wigs many a long day ago."

So he begins a-sayin' as he were for liberty.

"Ah!" I says, "so I've 'eard a many say, as means live in idleness and let others support you."

"Ah!" he says, "insult poverty, that's you, Mrs. Brown, all over."

I says, "'Ow do you know my name?"

"Why," he says, "I've seen you at my old friend, Mrs. Wrabbles."

"Oh!" I says, "I remember, you're the party

as called yourself the reasoner, as went into the book-line, tho' in the witriol works, cos you thought as you could take and enlighten the 'uman race by 'awkin' books, as was no better than blasfemin' in my opinion, and wuss than that some on 'em." I'd quite forgot 'im, for I 'adn't set eyes on 'im for years, and werry much changed for the wuss, he were, with a 'usky voice and a pimply nose, as is signs of suction, in my opinion; and when fust I see 'im he were good-lookin', tho' I 'adn't no consumption who he was then, as I 'appened to be a-goin' out one afternoon when he come up to the door, a werry civil-spoken young man, as were a-sellin' books, and wanted me for to take 'em in monthly parts, and I'm sure they was remarkable cheap to look at, so thought I'd buy some, for I likes to 'ave somethink to read; leastways for the gal to read to me, as is a pretty scholar, and I takes a interest in 'er, thro' a-takin' 'er a orfin, and promised as she shouldn't forget 'er learnin'; not as I 'olds with too much of that readin', as is all werry well of a evenin' for a recreation like, and she often do read to me for a bit when Brown's gone for a walk, or to smoke a pipe with a friend, as is 'is 'abits, partikler sometimes of a Sunday evenin' in summer time.

Well, this young man as was a-sellin' the books, he'd got one along with 'im as was about " Social

Science," so I says, " that's a book as I should like
to 'ave, for I'm sociable myself."

" Oh," he says, " it wouldn't suit you."

" No," I says, " it's too close printed for my
eyes, but I've got a young gal as lives along with
me as would read it to me."

" So," he says, " it ain't a book for 'er; you'd
better 'ave the ' Istory of England' in parts."

" No," I says, " I've done that afore, and only
took in five numbers, when they stopped it sudden,
jest afore comin' to Queen Elizabeth, as is a
party I wants to 'ear somethink about, thro' not
a-believin' in 'er myself, nor yet my good gentleman."

" Well," he says, " would you like the Pictorial
Bible ?"

" No," I says, " I've got one, as is enough for
me."

So at last I bought a sixpenny book on 'im, and
let 'im go.

That werry evenin' we was a-goin' to tea at the
Wrabbles', as is parties I've only know'd lately, and
Brown wouldn't go, thro' a-'atin' new acquaint-
ances.

We 'ad a nice tea enough, for they lives werry
nigh to the Clapham Junction, and you can see the
fireworks at Cremorne from the front winders.

I didn't much care for Mr. Wrabbles, as is a

man as 'll swear at a trifle, like 'is tea bein' too 'ot;
but of all the men as ever I did meet, it was that
same young feller as 'ad been a-tryin' to sell me
them books that werry day. I did stare when I see
'im walk in dressed werry flashy like, and is 'air
'iled, into Mrs. Wrabbles' parlour, as seemed werry
glad to see 'im. I were not quite sure as he could
be the same young man as that 'awker when he
come and set near me, as Mrs. Wrabbles said we
should jest suit one another, thro' bein' both
good talkers, and she says, " This is our dear old
friend, Mrs. Brown." Why, bless the woman, I
'adn't known 'er a month, and this, she says to
me, " Is a risin' young feller, tho' I says it afore
'im in the name of Wilks," as were a cousin of
Wrabbles'.

We got a-talkin' about books over tea, thro'
me a-sayin', jest to try if he were the same man,
as I'd bought a werry pretty tale at the door for
sixpence.

" Ah," he says, " some of them cantin' tracks,
as is all false."

I says, " They may be cantin', but," I says,
" as to bein' all false, they're not, for," I says,
" many on 'em is about what is true."

He says, " True; why, you ain't so soft as to
believe all that rubbish."

I says, " You're no doubt werry clever, and 'ave

studied werry deep, no doubt, as I know'd to be a likely chance, thro' Mrs. Wrabbles a-tellin' me about 'im only bein' employed on the witriol works."

" Oh," he says, " I'm a lecturer."

I says, " No doubt; and pray where did you learn anythink to lecture on ?"

" Oh," he says, " I've read a deal."

" Ah !" I says, " no doubt you must 'ave sich a deal of spare time for readin' as you walks along with 'em books to sell."

" Oh !" he says, " I 'aven't, and that's why I've give up my place in the works and took to books."

I says, " Oh, indeed !"

Mrs. Wrabbles, she says, " Law, Tom, you ain't been so foolish as to throw away two pounds a-week with a wife and family."

Wrabbles says, " What's two pound a-week to 'im as'll make 'undreds some day, and did ought to be in Parlyment."

Says Wilks to 'im, " Come, come, Joe, you are flatterin' me."

He says, " I ain't, you did ought to be there, and shall be too," and 'its the table that 'ard as he made the cups and sarcers ring agin.

I didn't say nothink, but set a-thinkin' what fools there is in this world, when in come Mrs. Wilks and a little boy, as said she couldn't come no sooner thro' 'avin' no one to leave the hinfant till 'er mother come in.

The moment I set eyes on 'er I see as she were one of 'em poor dragged-to-death creeturs, as their lives is reg'lar wore out of 'em.

We got a-talkin' on all manner, and she was a-sayin' as she'd berried a little boy only three weeks afore, and the tears come into 'er eyes.

So I says, " Never mind, he's better off."

Says Wilks, a-turnin' on me, " 'Ow do you know that ? "

Why, I says, " I've been told so by them as 'ave studied, and knows more about it than I do."

" Ah !" he says, " you'd believe anythink, you would."

" No," I says, "that I wouldn't, for I wouldn't believe your lectures, as I'm sure can't know nothink at all about what you're a-talkin' on." I says, " The idea of you, as 'ave passed best part of your life in writriol, a-knowin' anythink about 'em things as is a study for 'em as 'ave got more brains in their little fingers than you 'ave in your whole body, and give their lives to it."

I see poor Mrs. Wilks look at me, uneasy-like.

As to 'im, he got downright abusive, a-callin' me " A ignorant old thing as couldn't speak two words of English."

I says, " Pre'aps I can't, but if I can't speak

English I don't know what I do speak, for three
words of French is the outside of what I knows."

He says, "You don't know grammer."

I says, "You don't know manners to tell me
so; but," I says, "no doubt you're reg'lar upper-
crust in your own opinion; but," I says, "you
reminds me of a sheep's 'ead as is all jaw."

We was a-talkin' charfin' at fust, but was a-gettin' warm over it; so Mrs. Wrabbles, she changes
the subjec, and werry soon arter we left the gentlemen over their pipes while we went to 'ave a bit
of a talk with Mrs. Wrabbles, as were a-goin' to
give an eye to the supper.

So poor Mrs. Wilks, she says, "I'm glad as you
was down on my 'usband, as is that overbearin', and
won't let me 'ave the children christened nor nothink decent, and does go on so agin religion."

I says, "That shows 'is ignorance, for nobody
can't say as religion is a bad thing, so wherefore go
agin it in others if you don't like it yourself."

We'd a delicious supper of 'am and peas, and
everythink a-goin' nice, and jest as we was done I
was a-settin' quiet and Wilks begun at me, a-hol-
lerin' out as I were sayin' grace.

"Well," I says, "if I ain't I ought to be for
I've 'ad a capital supper," as made 'im toss 'is 'ead,
and say such superstishun made 'im sick.

"Well," I says, "I like that, whatever can it

matter to you? You can eat your wittles like a dog, if you likes, and nobody won't care." I says, "It's time for you to 'oller out when I says grace for you."

He went on a deal more, but I says, "Now, that's a good man, do smoke your pipe and drink your sperrits and water, as no doubt your thankful to Mrs. Wrabbles for, and pre'aps may come to want afore you die, tho' you are so grand over it."

"Ah!" he says, "I shall never want."

"Well," I says, "I 'ope not. I didn't come 'ere to talk religion, as is everybody's own affair, but to spend a pleasant evenin', so let's drop it." And I begun a-talkin' about all manner; but do you think as that man would let it alone, not 'im, for he kep' a-goin' on till I was that wild as I wouldn't stop no longer, and 'ome I goes.

I 'ad the Wrabbles back to tea six weeks arter when Brown was away, and she told me as things was a-goin' werry quisby with 'em Wilkses.

I says, "I'm sorry for 'er, but he's a party I don't 'old with, as in my opinion deserves to want, only but for others as would want with 'im."

She says, "He's been and got 'isself in a 'ole with them books as he've been lewanted with, and will get two years over it, they say," and so he did, and I never 'eard nor see 'im till I met 'im in that crowd.

So he says, "You're the same old bigot as ever, I suppose."

I says, "And you're the same blusterous party as ever."

"Ah!" he says, "wait till we gets a reg'lar Liberal Government in, and not a sham like Gladstin's."

"Ah!" I says, "and then we shall all be a-cuttin' one another's throats, like them Communists over in Paris."

"Hurrah!" says a man, "well done, old lady! let's 'ave a speech."

I says, "I ain't one to make no speeches."

"Hurrah!" says another; "she's come for to adwocate woman's suffrage. Let's 'ear wot she's got to say."

"'Elp 'er on to the lamp-post," says one; "bring out a tub for 'er to stand on."

"Let me alone," says I.

Up comes three perlice, and took and collared me.

I says, "Perlice, 'ow dare you! I'll report you, see if I don't." But law, for all as I could say they walked me off afore the magistret, as told me if I'd got any grievance, as I did ought to 'ave it set right in a proper way, and not go a-kickin' up a row about Parlyment, as wasn't lorful.

I says, "Your worship, it were the last of my thoughts, as were only a-speakin'."

" Yes," he says, "but you mustn't speak in the public streets; so now go 'ome quietly, with a caution."

Well, 'ome I went, leastways to Mrs. Padwick's, 'arf dead, and there she was a-waitin' tea, and wonderin' wotever 'ad become on me, cos she went and got into a bus, a-thinkin' as I were a-follerin', when the crowd took and parted us. I was that wexed and put out, to think as I should be treated like that, and I were a-sayin' to Mrs. Padwick, "I'm sure if Queen Wictorier only knowed one-'arf of wot is goin' on, she'd feel werry different to wot she does, and not be able to set a-smilin' and a-bowin' in 'er open carridge, cos," I says, " mark my words, as them Radicals, as is only a set of idle waggerbones, will try to upset everythink;" and, I says, "I remembers werry well a old feller as lived out Battersea way, as were werry old when I were quite a child, as 'ad been one for Wilks and liberty."

"Ah!" says, Mrs. Padwick, " I've 'eard say as he were a bold, bad man, that Wilks," as were Lord Mare afore he died, for all that, as made King George tremble afore 'im, and such insults to Queen Charlotte, as they reg'lar mobbed a-comin' 'ome from Lord Mare's show, as showed a proper sperrit, and put 'er 'ead out of the winder, and give it 'em 'ot, in broken English, as she never 'adn't learnt, tho' she was Queen of Ingland over fifty years, as made 'em ashamed of theirselves, and slunk away, and so the old lady got 'ome in peace, as 'adn't no sich time on it even there with sich a rantypole lot of children, as were that cheeky, as they do say when old King George were a-correctin' 'is eldest boy, as were called Prince of Wales, if the owdacious young willin didn't take and cry "Wilks and liberty!" under 'is royal father's nose.

I'm sure I wish I 'adn't thought of Wilks nor liberty neither, for I got a-dreamin' all night as Dizzy were turned into Wilks and 'ad been made Lord Mare, as Queen Wictorier 'ad ordered his 'ead to be chopped off for tryin' to steal the crown out of the Tower, and as Gladstin 'ad been in the swim, and then been and rounded on 'im, as were a despisable hact; but the Prince of Wales he got 'im off thro' bein' that good natured as can't a-bear cruelty to animals, and jest as Queen Wictorier were a-goin' to tell me wot she were a-goin' to do when the Hemperor of Roosher come, I woke up, and it was jest time to get up, so up I gets a-sayin' no more dreams this side of bed time for me.